# THIS SIDE OF PARADISE

From the start Gina and her so-called friend Marie were at cross-purposes about their holiday in the Bahamas. Marie was unashamedly after a rich man; Gina just wanted a once-in-a-life-time holiday. But when Ryan Barras got entirely the wrong idea about her, it didn't stop Gina from falling in love with him. How could she make him change his mind about her?

KAY THORPE

# THIS SIDE OF PARADISE

*Complete and Unabridged*

# LINFORD
*Leicester*

First published in Great Britain 1979 by
Mills & Boon Ltd
London

First Large Print Edition
published February 1985
by arrangement with
Mills & Boon Ltd
London

9/90 Ulveis. 5.60

British Library CIP Data

Thorpe, Kay
   This side of paradise.—Large print ed.—
(Linford romance library)
I. Title
823′.914[F]        PR6070.H69/

ISBN 0-7089-6057-X

Published by
F. A. Thorpe (Publishing) Ltd.
Anstey, Leicestershire
Set by Rowland Phototypesetting Ltd.
Bury St. Edmunds, Suffolk
Printed and bound in Great Britain by
T. J. Press (Padstow) Ltd., Padstow, Cornwall

# 1

THE blonde in the yellow bikini caught the eye of the paunchy, balding man in Bermuda shorts seated at one of the poolside tables, and smiled a smile of invitation. Without moving from his seat or changing expression, the man lifted a finger and indicated the chair at his side, using the same finger to beckon a waiter as the girl sauntered over.

Watching the bit of by-play from their third floor balcony, Gina wondered dryly if Marie had realised that financial security all too rarely went hand in glove with youth and good looks in places like this. She had taken it as a joke at first on the plane coming over when the other had announced her intention, but now she wasn't so sure. What did she really know about Marie Gregory apart from the fact that like herself she was on her own in the

1

world? Working alongside someone only provided insight into certain facets of character, not the whole conglomerate. There was every chance that Marie really had set out to save for this once-in-a-lifetime holiday with the sole purpose of snaring herself a rich husband.

Two years it had taken her, she had said. Two long frugal years before she had enough put by for one grand, three-week splurge. Gina was sure she could never have been as single-minded as that, no matter what the incentive. She owed her own presence here in the Bahamas to a friendly computer called Ernie and nothing else.

That Premium Bond win had provided a discussion point for the office for several days. Many and varied had been suggestions regarding the use to which she should put her thousand pounds, but Marie's had been the only one to hold any real appeal. Some had said she was a fool to spend the whole lot at once in such a way, while others had egged her on to snatch at the chance to see how the other half lived. Oddly enough it had never once occurred to her to ask Marie why she suddenly found herself in need of a companion on what had apparently been intended as a lone trip. Not, at least, until they were on the plane and it was too late to back out.

Standing here now, barely eight hours later, she remembered the little smile with which Marie had received the question and her disconcerting answer. "I needed a foil," she had added, as if that explained everything. Gina still wasn't sure just what that meant, although she supposed her own fairness did add a certain subtle emphasis to Marie's dark vivacity. They had attracted a fair amount of attention down in the lobby on arrival, perhaps not least because they appeared to be in a minority where youth was concerned. Gina had never seen so many blue-rinsed women and ageing men together in one place before. Not that the hotel was full —it was too pre-season for that.

Lifting her eyes from their contemplation of the pool below, she looked out across the casuarinas to the stretch of white beach lapped by a sea turning opaque in the fading light. Tomorrow there would be time to sample the delights of swimming in a warmth no European waters could match, or lying in the hot sun under a cloudless blue sky and doing nothing for hours on end. For tonight, there was dinner down in the luxurious restaurant to look forward to, although so far as her inner clock was concerned it was still only lunchtime as yet. No doubt it took a little time to adjust to a five-hour time difference. A good night's sleep would probably help.

"Are you going to come and finish unpacking?" came Marie's voice from within the room. "I want to know how much space I've got for my things."

"Take as much as you need. I didn't bring as many." Gina turned with reluctance and left the balcony, stepping back into the large, beautifully furnished room with a swift renewal of pleasure. "Isn't this just fabulous? I feel like a millionairess!"

"It isn't bad," Marie admitted. "And neither should it be for the price we're paying. Thank God for cheap air fares!"

Gina echoed the sentiment mentally, aware that without them even her thousand would not have sufficed. As it was, the fare plus allowance for the hotel charges had made a big hole in her resources. She only hoped she was going to have enough traveller's cheques to last out the three weeks, taking into consideration that they had to buy their meals as well as entertainment. Still, tonight wasn't the time to start worrying about money. It was their first.

Marie was wearing a bra and brief set which left little to the imagination. She had a superb figure which she dressed to emphasise. Gina admired her looks without particular envy. Her own slender shape might not be as spectacular, but neither was her personality, and a body like Marie's needed living up to. At least no one could mistake her for a boy, she thought with humour, catching a glimpse of herself in the dressing mirror.

"What time is dinner?" she asked.

"We'll go down about nine," Marie said.

"Not until then? I'm feeling hungry now."

"Your own fault. You should have eaten lunch on the plane."

"We'd only just had breakfast—or that's what it felt like." The argument was in no way serious, it was just something to say. Sharing a room with someone she knew as superficially as she knew Marie wasn't going to be as easy as she had thought—if she had thought about it at all. Their friendship had only really begun at the moment three weeks ago when she had accepted the invitation to accompany her here. Friendship? Relationship might be a better word. Marie made little effort to extend herself in any direction but the one which suited her.

She finished her unpacking, leaving as much space as she could for Marie's things, then fingered through the dresses she had brought with an indecisive air.

"Are you wearing long or short?" she asked over her shoulder.

"Long, of course. It's the place for it." Marie reached across her to pick out a shaded blue crêpe with narrow straps and a shaped top. "Wear that, it brings up your eyes. Pity you didn't have a rinse on your hair before we came. Ash blonde would look great with a tan." Her glance was assessing. "You don't make the most of yourself, you know."

"I'm not the one who's after a husband," Gina came back lightly, refusing to take offence.

There was a hint of contempt in the reply. "I suppose you'll be content to settle for some struggling little bank clerk, and finish up with hordes of kids hanging on to your skirts!"

Gina had to smile. "You paint such a pretty picture. It doesn't have to happen like that."

"It will to you. You're the type."

There was a pause as she turned away. Gina was the first to break it. "Marie, why did you ask me to come with you?"

7

The other shrugged. "Because a woman on her own in a place like this can give the wrong impression—attract the wrong type."

"Then all you really need is to establish the fact that we're here together and we can both go our own ways, can't we?"

"No reason why not." Her voice was indifferent. "Some people you can't help."

That kind of help she could do without, Gina reflected dryly. Not for anything was she going to be sorry she had come, though. This was a once-in-a-lifetime trip and she was going to make the most of it —but in her own way. Let Marie do as she liked providing she didn't involve her.

They went down together on the hour, one in blue, the other in a deep tawny orange which made the most of her colouring. Marie created a minor sensation crossing the opulent entrance lounge; Gina could see the heads turning to look and knew she was not the recipient.

The restaurant was little more than half full, its big terrace doors flung wide on the view of the moon-spangled sea. On a

8

raised dais towards the rear of the room a band was playing selections from the latest musicals, and one or two couples were dancing. The keynote was quiet luxury, from the silk drapes and velvet-covered chairs right down to the last gleaming piece of silver.

Seated at a table on the far side of the dance floor, Gina was conscious that her own dress bore no comparison with the expensive fashions around her. Neither did Marie's if it came to that, but it didn't seem to bother her. She had confidence enough to hold her own with anyone. Right then Gina wished she had a little more herself.

There were a few other younger people present, she noted, but hardly the kind one made casual acquaintances of. Mostly they looked bored half to death, as if this kind of evening was an all too common occurrence—which it probably was for them. She and Marie were the only two females without escorts that she could see, and that hardly helped. For the first time she began to realise that this was the wrong kind of hotel for the type of holiday she had planned in her mind. She needed somewhere smaller, more casual, if such places existed on New Providence. But it was too late now.

Her first glance down the menu brought a small sound of dismay to her lips. The prices were exorbitant even for the minor items. If they ate here in the hotel all the time her reserve of cash would last her about a week at the outside.

Marie told the waiter they would order later, and asked for two Martinis to be brought to the table.

"Stop worrying," she said when Gina confided her fears. "If you play your cards right you won't need buy any dinners after tonight."

"You mean find someone to buy them for me instead?"

"On the nail. There's a man off to your left who's been giving you the eye ever since you walked in."

Involuntarily, Gina turned her head to the left, to find herself looking straight at the same man she had watched on the pool terrace earlier. The blonde who had joined him then was sitting with him now, but he appeared to be paying her little attention. A big thick cigar sat between the thick fleshy lips, regardless of the fact that they were only partway through their meal. The white tuxedo served only to emphasise the rolls of fat at the back of his neck.

"No, thanks," she said with a shudder, looking hastily away again. "Anyway, he already has a partner."

"She's not a day under thirty, and not exactly holding his attention. I'd say he'll be ditching her before long."

"Then why don't *you* try to capture his attention?" Gina hissed angrily, and saw the other girl smile.

"I don't fancy him either. Now there's a couple out on the terrace—men, I mean —who look a far better bet. I wonder if they're staying here or just eating out of town?"

"Go and ask them." Gina had had enough. The whole thing was turning into a fiasco. She supposed if the truth were

11

known, she had never really got far beyond the actual journeying here in her imaginings. Certainly she had never anticipated feeling so completely out of her depth.

Marie shrugged. "There's no hurry. If they're not resident it's hardly worth engineering a meeting. We'll find out tomorrow."

Despite herself, Gina wondered just how Marie would have gone about that particular task. From where she sat she couldn't see the two men, and had no intention of looking. If they were staying here and Marie did manage to become acquainted, she would make sure she stayed as far away as possible from the whole affair. She would simply have to eke her money out, that was all. Bathing in the sea and sitting on the sand could hardly cost anything. And there must be some cheaper places to eat.

When they finally got round to ordering she deliberately chose the least expensive items she could find, but even then, according to her reckoning, the bill for her meal alone came to more than seven pounds sterling. Marie showed no such frugality, ordering what she fancied, along with a bottle of wine.

"It's on me," she said when Gina protested. "Stop being so wet!"

"I'm sorry," Gina said, flushing a little. "I only have about two hundred pounds to last me out. Seventy pounds a week seemed ample back home, but I can't see it going very far out here."

"I don't have much more myself," Marie rejoined calmly. "And I don't intend spending any more of that than I have to. If you weren't such a little fool you could have a great time without worrying about a thing."

"I may be a fool, but I'm not putting myself on the market for a cheap meal ticket!" Gina flashed back.

"Neither am I." Marie sounded unperturbed. "You know what I'm after. But I have to live between times."

Gina cast a glance about her. "You'll never find a husband here. I doubt if the marrying types come to places like this."

"You could easily be right. Marriage isn't everything." Marie watched Gina's change of expression with a lift of her brows. "You must have realised by now that I'm not going back unless I absolutely have to. If I can't get a husband to keep me in the style I'd like to become accustomed to, I'll settle for what I can get. All I ask is that he's loaded."

Gina was staring at her as if she had never seen her before, which she hadn't—at least not in any depth. "You can't mean that!"

"Of course I mean it. I didn't scrimp and save for two years for nothing."

"Then why drag me along?"

"I told you. I thought it would look better initially."

"Being alone doesn't appear to bother that woman over there with the man you pointed out to me. She picked him up this afternoon down by the pool."

"She's obviously on the make, and I don't want to look that way. So far as the record goes, we're two friends taking a vacation together. Of course, if I give you

14

the nod I'll expect you to float off and find your own company."

Gina shook her head, struggling for equanimity. "I suppose it's your life and you've a perfect right to do what you want with it. but don't expect me to help you out. Like I said upstairs, we'll each go our own way."

Marie smiled. "You're going to get awfully lonely." That was true, and the thought held little appeal.

But the alternative held less. She wasn't going to let this spoil things, Gina told herself fiercely. She was in the Bahamas for the sun, the sea and the sand, and those were what she would concentrate on enjoying.

She didn't enjoy her meal when it came, despite the cost—or because of it, she wasn't sure which. Marie drank most of the wine, without apparent effect except for an added glint in her dark eyes. She ordered crème de menthe to go with her coffee, and sat sipping it and tapping her foot lightly in time to the music, watching

15

the dancers moving slowly around the floor.

"I suppose there'll be three times as many here in high season," she remarked at one point.

"I imagine there will," Gina agreed wearily. "Why didn't you wait and come then?"

"Because I couldn't wait to save enough." Marie's eyes lifted beyond Gina's head and changed expression. "Remember those two out on the terrace I mentioned? One of them looks as if he might be coming over. Don't go and spoil things."

Gina felt herself stiffen as a white tuxedo hove into view from behind her chair, but the man wearing it had eyes only for Marie. He was medium height and only a little overweight, with a not unpleasant set of features beneath a full head of hair. He looked around the mid-forties.

"Forgive the intrusion," he said easily. "My friend and I wondered if you'd consider joining us for a drink on the terrace. We seem to be the odd men out tonight."

Marie gave him a smile which held no hint of provocation. "Or women, as the case may be." The hesitation was beautifully done. "It's very nice of you, but I don't really think . . ."

"Please do." His own smile had charm. "You'd be easing a rather awkward situation. I invited an old pal out for what turned out to be a very dull meal." His glance had moved to Gina, brows quizzically tilted. "As fellow Britishers?"

"How did you know we were English?" she asked, despite herself.

"One learns to recognise one's own. I'm Neil Davids, by the way."

Marie made the necessary introductions, her glance quelling Gina's attempt to bring in some excuse for not taking things any further. "We only got in this afternoon and we're both feeling the time difference, so I'm afraid we won't be able to stay too long," she said, as if just making up her mind.

"Fine. Whatever you say."

17

Marie was already rising, leaving Gina with little else to do but follow suit. She didn't want to go with this man, but neither did she fancy crossing the room on her own if she refused, because it was pretty certain that Marie would not be coming with her.

The terrace doors were only a few feet away, the table for which they were heading occupied by a man at present gazing seaward with a set look about the broad shoulders under the well cut white jacket. When he turned his dark head, Gina saw at once that this had not been his idea. There was resignation in his expression, as if he had been overridden by a will stronger than his own—except that wills didn't come much stronger, she would have thought, than that implicit in the line of his jaw. A strongly boned face, and one which to her at least was familiar enough to bring his name involuntarily to her lips.

"Ryan Barras!"

"Your fame seeks you out," said the

other man at her back on a faintly wry note.

"So it seems." Grey eyes considered her coolly as he came to his feet. "I'm flattered, Miss . . . ?"

He was anything but, and she knew it. What was more, he knew that she knew it. "Tierson," she supplied stiffly. "Gina Tierson."

"And this is Marie." Neil Davids sounded hearty, obviously aware that he had made something of a gaffe. "They only got in a few hours ago." He saw them seated, placing Gina next to the terrace wall and right across from the sardonic grey eyes, and himself taking the seat at her side so that he could look at Marie without turning his head.

The waiter he summoned was deferential in a manner which left them in no doubt as to their host's standing, addressing him as Mr. Davids. As he departed to fill the order, Marie said brightly, "I gather you already know Mr. Barras, Gina?"

"Know of," he corrected her, his eyes

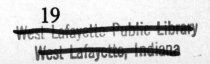

never leaving Gina's face. "Are you an avid reader, Miss Tierson?"

"Here, we're all supposed to be British," Neil cut in. "Let's drop the formality, shall we?"

His companion shrugged. "All right then, are you an avid reader—Gina?" The pause was fleeting. "Short for Virginia?"

"Yes," she said. "And yes to the other question too." She forced herself to meet his gaze levelly. "I suppose you're sick of people telling you they've read all your books."

"Not at all. I'm as narcissistic as the next one when it comes to my work." The irony was as much self-directed. "Hardback?"

"Mostly. Your photograph was inside the jacket of the last two, and I saw you on television a few months ago."

"You've a good memory for faces."

His was hard to forget, Gina reflected. Along with that manner of his too. She recalled the way he had put the TV interviewer in his place with a few well chosen words when the questioning

20

had verged too close to the intimate. Something to do with the current woman in his life, if she remembered correctly. At thirty-four he had apparently known quite a few pretty well. Unmarried, and intending to stay that way by all accounts.

The others had started their own conversation, although Marie's ears were pricked for anything of interest, she noted. She wished she was far away from here, far away from this man whose regard held such knowledgeable derision. She felt cheapened by that look, and deserving of it too.

"So aren't you going to tell me how you enjoyed my writing?" he asked on a note of irony. "Which did you like best?"

"*The Hunters*," she said, and saw his brows lift. "I shouldn't have thought that held much appeal for a woman."

"Do you write for men only?" she challenged.

"Not consciously perhaps, but the subject matter is male-orientated."

"Only on the surface. Some traits are common to both sexes."

"Too true." There was an element of

interest in his expression. "Mind me asking how old you are?"

"Twenty-three," she said. "More than old enough to understand what you were getting at in that particular novel."

He smiled a little. "It's three years since *The Hunters* was published."

"I only started reading you a few months ago," she confessed. "I caught up with your other books through the public library."

"And there I was thinking I'd found a hardback buyer!"

"At five pounds or so a time it comes rather expensive." She could immediately have bitten off her tongue. Lack of money was a subject one did not discuss in places like this. She could feel her face warming.

"Find a way of cutting down printing costs and you'd have the publishing world at your feet," he came back dryly. "My next one out is going on the market at five seventy-five, and they won't hold that for long."

"When is it due?"

"Middle of next month. Would you like an advance copy?"

"Oh no!" she protested, then stopped, flustered by the tilt of his lips. "I mean that would be marvellous, of course, but I don't expect . . ."

"That's all right. A fan is worth cultivating." He took out a gold pen and a wallet with a small memo pad inside it, looked back at her expectantly. "Tell me where to send it."

She did so reluctantly, sensing his reaction to the address.

"You'll be home by then?" he asked.

"Yes."

"So this is just a vacation."

"Yes," she said again. Marie was listening, and obviously not liking the turn the conversation had taken, but there was nothing she could do about it.

Ryan was watching her with a certain calculation. "It's a long way to come for a couple of weeks."

"Three," she said, and immediately felt ridiculous. "I suppose it is, but it's worth it." She saw his lips twist again and added hurriedly, "It's such a beautiful part of the world, isn't it? Are you staying here long yourself?"

"I live here," he said. "At least for three months of the year."

"While you write your books?"

"That's right. I need seclusion when I'm writing."

She forced a smile. "I'd have thought that rather difficult in Nassau."

"I don't stay in Nassau." He made no attempt to add to the statement, leaning back as the waiter arrived with their drinks.

"What shall we drink to?" asked Neil lightly when the latter had departed, and Marie laughed.

"We're all English, how about Queen and Country?"

"Too impersonal. How about friend-ships—old and new?"

She lifted her glass, eyes holding his with a look of shared understanding behind the laughter. "I'll go along with that."

Ryan didn't touch his glass. Like Gina

he just left it standing there. The smell of cigar smoke mingled with perfume took over even out here, but nothing could disguise the balmy warmth of the night air on the skin or the sparkling clarity of the stars up there in a sky completely free of industrial haze. A week ago she had only been dreaming about this, and now here she was. Why couldn't it be the same?

"Would you like to walk down to the beach?" Ryan asked. His tone was casual. "I don't suppose you've had much time yet to go very far."

There were other couples strolling down there among the casuarinas. Anything, Gina thought, would be better than sitting here struggling to hold up her end to Marie's specifications.

"Yes," she said. "I would, please."

"How about you two?" turning to Neil with a bare glance in Marie's direction.

The other man smiled and shook his head. "We're going to dance." He stood up to pull back Gina's chair for her, staying on his feet as Ryan came round the table to join her, a mocking light in his eyes. "See you in a while."

There were steps leading down from the terrace to the gardens immediately adjoining. Ryan went down them a little ahead of her, stopping at the bottom to let her catch up. He was about six feet in height, she judged, and built like an athlete, the broad shoulders tapering down to narrow hips. She felt a sudden swift tensing of muscle and sinew that had nothing to do with nerves—unless attraction came under that heading. Well, she wasn't the first to find him attractive, and there was no doubt she wouldn't be the last. The thought unaccountably depressed her.

He made no effort to reopen conversation, seemingly content to stroll at her side with hands thrust into trouser pockets. Down here the night scents came through thickly. A light breeze caught at the smooth cap of her hair, lifting strands which glinted silver in the moonlight.

"You should have brought a wrap," he said suddenly, and she laughed.

"Not on a night like this, surely!"

"It's cool by local standards. This is the low season, you know."

"I know. The hurricane season, according to the literature I read."

"Couldn't you make it later?"

"Couldn't afford it later. It had . . ." She stopped abruptly, once more aware of having said too much. Yet why should it matter to her? Where was the point in trying to seem what she was not?

They had reached the path down through the palms to the beach proper. For the moment they appeared to have it to themselves.

"You're playing a dangerous game," he said on a hard note. "I daresay you know that too."

Her breath caught. "I'm . . . not sure what you mean."

"Don't take me for a complete fool. You're here on holiday in a place you obviously can't afford, and the only way you're going to see your way is through those who can."

"That's not true!" She stopped walking

and swung towards him, face set and angry. "You don't . . ."

"I understand all right—only too well. It happens all the time. I'm not saying you won't succeed. You're young and attractive—and intelligent." His mouth curled. "Too intelligent, I'd have thought, to get caught up in something like this. How the devil did you get mixed up with the other one?"

His tone made her bridle. "If you mean Marie, don't talk about her like that!"

"She's on the make," he said bluntly. "It's as plain as daylight."

"*Your* friend didn't seem to think so."

The laugh was short. "Neil knows an easy score when he sees one. Not that he won't be prepared to come through for it. She might even be set for the whole three weeks if she plays her cards right."

Gina flared, driven by shame as much as anger. Her hand came up in an arc towards the lean face, only to be caught and held in a grip which made her cry out.

"Don't count on me turning the other

cheek," he said. "It wouldn't be the first time I'd slapped a woman back!"

"That doesn't surprise me!" She tore her hand free with a strength which surprised them both, clutching her wrist where his fingers had bruised the flesh. "What gives you the right to judge others?"

"I'm not judging, I'm warning. What your friend gets up to is her affair. I'd say she's more than capable of taking care of herself."

"And you think I'm not."

"I'm sure of it. You're going to get yourself into a spot there's only one way out of." He paused with deliberation. "Unless you don't mind paying for your supper in a strange bed? Maybe I'm preaching to a lost cause."

"Swine!" The word choked her. Tears of humiliation prickled behind her lids. She turned to go, stumbling as her foot caught on an edging stone and flinging out a defending hand to ward off the one he thrust out to catch her. "Don't touch me. I don't need *your* help!"

"You need something," he said grimly. "I'm not sure what." He spun her round to face him again, looking down into her angry face with a slow change of expression. "Maybe this will help to convince you how far you're equipped to handle what you're asking for!"

She tensed as he pulled her up to him, feeling the hardness of his body crushing the breath from her. His mouth was ruthless, forcing her lips apart, his hands moving down over her. She had never been kissed with such brutality before in her life. When he let her go she couldn't look at him, backing away with a hand pressed against her bruised lips.

"That was only a sample," he said. "It could get a whole lot rougher if you try playing fast and loose with some of the characters you might meet in these parts. Still think you can cope?"

"I never said I wanted to cope." She was trembling, her mouth on fire, her whole body seeming to bear the imprint of those steel-like fingers. "You had no right to do that!"

"You needed it. If you've any sense at all you'll benefit from it. How much money do you actually have?"

"Enough to prove you wrong!"

"I hope so."

"Why should you care anyway?" she demanded, fighting the urgent desire to burst into tears. "You don't even know me!"

"Put it down to the last remnants of gallantry left in me." He studied her, face hard in the moonlight. "Ready to go back?"

"I'll take myself back."

"No, you won't. I have to go that way to get a cab."

She said unsteadily, "What about your friend? I thought you came together."

"We did. That doesn't mean I'm going to break up whatever he's got going for him to get back to town."

"I told you . . ."

"I know what you told me. About that you won't convince me. I've seen too many of her type to make any mistakes."

A cutting remark trembled on Gina's

lips, but she bit it back. Not for anything would she risk a repeat of the last few minutes. Whatever attraction Ryan had held for her had flown. All she felt now was detestation. The way he had kissed her, the way he had held her—there had been no need for that. He had deliberately degraded her, like some common little tramp.

They reached the terrace again in silence. There was no sign of the others. Ryan retrieved Gina's purse from the table where they had been sitting and handed it to her, then accompanied her through the restaurant and out into the entrance lounge. If Marie and Neil were dancing she didn't see them because she didn't care to look. Not with Ryan's eyes on her.

He stopped opposite the lifts, expression enigmatic. "I guess this is where we say goodbye. I can't say it's been a pleasant evening, because it hasn't particularly. If you do happen to see Neil you might tell him I've gone back to the boat."

"I'm going up to my room," she said. "So I shan't be seeing him."

"Just a thought." The smile held cynicism. "Try to remember what I told you. You're not cut out for this game."

Gina didn't answer. It wasn't worth it. She turned from him and walked across to the lifts, pressing the button with a finger that felt nerveless. Fortunately it came almost at once. She didn't look back as the doors slid silently closed behind her.

The bedroom was unoccupied. But of course it would be. Marie was hardly likely to let things get that far this soon—if she ever really intended to let them get that far at all. Gina tried to convince herself and knew she failed. Ryan was right about Marie if about nothing else. What he didn't know was that she planned on staying far longer than the three weeks he had spoken of, given the opportunity. Whether Neil Davids would be the means of her staying was open to chance. Ryan apparently knew him well enough to consider three weeks a distinct possibility, so why not longer?

Her mouth still looked swollen when she viewed it in the mirror, her eyes dark.

Attractive, Ryan had called her. She supposed she should be grateful for his condescension. Right now she felt like packing her things and getting out of this place for good. Except that she couldn't, could she? They were booked on a flight structure which allowed no leeway for chopping and changing dates. She was stuck here for three weeks whether she liked it or not.

So enjoy it, she told herself fiercely. Forget tonight and Ryan Barras, and just enjoy it!

She was in bed but still awake when Marie finally came up. The other switched on the lights regardless, closing the door and standing there for a moment with a satisfied little smile on her face before realising that Gina was there before her.

"I thought you'd gone off with that writer," she exclaimed in surprise. "How long have you been in bed?"

"About an hour," Gina said. She made no attempt to sit up, lying on her back with her eyes on the ceiling. "How did you get on?"

"Fine. He's quite a guyl"

"Are you seeing him again?"

"Not for a week, unfortunately—he has some business on the mainland. But he'll be back." She sounded supremely confident of that. "How about you? Are you seeing Ryan again?"

"No." The word was flat.

"Too bad. You seemed to have something going there. Are you sure he won't be back?"

"I'm sure. And I don't want to talk about it."

"Oh, I see. Like that, is it?" Marie laughed. "Attractive devil, I'll grant you, if you like the type. Personally I found him a bit too much. Men like that are okay in small doses, but they tend to want things too much their own way. Now Neil is a gentleman, he doesn't rush it. I could even fall for him a little."

"Do it." Gina rolled over on her stomach. "Just leave me out of it, that's all."

"Oh, don't worry, I will. I didn't expect to have that kind of luck on the first night." Marie paused, said on a consoling note, "Cheer up, you'll feel different tomorrow. You can go and have that swim you've been rabbiting on about."

That was something, Gina reflected into the pillows. The holiday had only just begun.

# 2

**D**URING the course of the next couple of days Gina found plenty of reason to convince herself that she had not after all made such a mistake in coming to the Bahamas. The weather, the coastal scenery, the sheer difference of it all combined to recreate the initial wonder and delight.

The two of them took a trip into Nassau and spent a day shopping—mostly looking in Gina's case—in the busy, traffic-crowded centre. Gina loved the fringed surreys drawn by straw-hatted horses, the deep ting-tong of the Bermuda carriage bells. They ate lunch at one of the awning-shaded pavement cafés, drinking Bacardi and Coke through straws. Marie could be good company when she wasn't, as Gina privately put it, keeping an eye open to the future. She seemed content to wait until Neil Davids returned from his business trip before putting out any further feelers.

One thing she did refuse to do was bathe in the sea, although she was perfectly willing to sit around the pool in the briefest of bikinis and bask in the attention she drew. There was water skiing from the hotel landing stage, with an instructor provided. Gina would have liked to try it, but the cost was too high. Already her slender reserves were dwindling at an alarming rate, and they weren't even halfway through the first week yet. But she refused to let money problems occupy too much of her thoughts. She would get through—and not Marie's way either.

The latter had drifted down to the beach with her on their third afternoon, her figure shown to every advantage in a black net bikini which had solid inserts only where necessity dictated. Gina's own blue one was the briefest she had ever worn, but beside the other she felt almost over-dressed. They bought drinks at the beach bar, and found loungers under the shade of the trees. Both had acquired a light, even tan turning deeper every day, but the sun was too hot to lie in for long.

"Super boat coming in," Marie murmured lazily, watching the shimmering sea through dark glasses. "Haven't seen that before."

"It isn't one of the hotel's," Gina agreed, following her gaze. "Look at that heat haze! It's hotter than ever today."

"I heard someone say the glass was dropping, though." Marie had sat up a little, interest aroused as the launch came nosing in to the stage and a rope was thrown.

The two men who came ashore were young and blond-haired, dressed almost identically in jeans and tee-shirts. Both wore dark glasses through which they scanned the whole beach as they strolled towards the bar. Marie was a certain draw, and she didn't fail this time. The moment the two had glasses in their hands they made a beeline for where she and Gina were sitting.

"Hi," the first one greeted casually.

"Looks cool under here. Mind if we join you?"

"Help yourselves," Marie invited. "Nice boat you've got there."

"Sure is." He sat down beside her, pushing up the sunglasses to reveal a pair of confident blue eyes. "Nice view you've got here."

The other man took the lounger on Gina's far side, making her feel they were being hemmed in. They were both in their late twenties, she judged, and one of them, at least, had American blood in his veins.

"I'm Sven, he's Rafe," he announced. "Are you both English?"

"Yes," she said. "Sven? That's Swedish, isn't it?"

"That's right." His accent was barely pronounced.

He showed white teeth in a brief grin. "But I'm no vegetable, honey."

She laughed. "I'll promise not to call you a Swede if you'll not call me that."

"It's a bargain. What else can I call you?"

She told him, relaxing under his easy manner. "Nice," he said.

Rafe called across one of the bar boys. "Refills all round," he said. "Bacardi, was it?"

"Just Coke for me, please," Gina broke in, and received a good-humoured grimace.

"A tot of rum won't hurt you."

"I know," she said. "I just prefer Coke during the day. "Drink less in the day, keep cirrhosis at bay," drawled Sven lazily. "Maybe we should try it too, Rafe."

"You try it, I'll choose my own road to ruin." The American eyed Marie with a tilt of his brows. "You're not on the wagon too, are you?"

"Not a chance." She was smiling, appraising the good-looking face with unconcealed approval. "Make mine a double."

"Which of you does the boat belong to?" asked Gina. It was Rafe who answered. "You could say we share it." He paused. "Like a run in her?"

"I wasn't hinting," she disclaimed hurriedly. Marie gave her an exasperated glance. "Well, if you wouldn't, I would."

41

"Well, that's great." He looked at Sven as if for confirmation, then added easily, "We're on our way to a party. Why not join us?"

Marie laughed. "Like this?"

"Sure. It's a beach party. They'll all be dressed like that—right, Sven?"

"Right. Good idea. You'd be welcomed with open arms."

"Is it close?"

"Close enough. We can have you back here in time for dinner, if that's what you want. They're a great crowd. You'll like them."

"Cocktails on the sand." Marie looked across to Gina, mouth tilting. "Sounds worth the trip."

"I don't think . . ." Gina began doubtfully, and received a derisive gesture.

"Don't be such a stick-in-the-mud! It's only for an hour or two. It's about time we had ourselves some fun." Confidently she turned back to Rafe. "I'll come anyway."

Sven leaned forward to place his empty

glass on the sand. "So will Gina, won't you?" His tone was pleasantly persuasive. "No fun staying here on your own."

Especially considering the fact that that left to her own devices, Marie might well decide to give dinner a miss altogether and leave her alone all evening as well, Gina conceded with a sense of resignation. At least if she were with her she could insist on returning to the hotel before dark. And a beach party did sound fun. A chance to meet some younger people perhaps; to see how the residents lived.

"All right," she said. "Providing it isn't too far."

The two men exchanged brief glances. "Let's get off now, then," said Rafe. "The sooner we set off the sooner we get there." He came to his feet, tossing a couple of notes on to the tray borne by the approaching bar boy. "We shan't be needing those now. Have yourself a ball."

The Nassauvian grinned. "Yassuh!"

Both girls had matching jackets to their suits. They slipped them on to make the short journey down to the landing stage,

Gina with a certain reluctance. The whole thing had happened so quickly she had barely had time to adjust. But holiday friendships were like that, weren't they? This kind, at any rate. If the invitation seemed casual it was probably because that was the way it was done round here.

The launch had a small cabin for'ard containing a couple of bench berths with lockers beneath. There was also a table which swung up from the bulkhead between, and a two-ring stove mounted on gimbals and run off Calor gas. Everything looked sparkling clean and new, the brasswork gleaming in the sunlight.

There was more seating lining the cockpit well. Taking a place beside Marie on the thick cushions, Gina tried to relax and anticipate the good time to come. She could hardly start backing out now, she told herself. She had agreed to go to this party and she was going to darn well enjoy it.

Yet something about the two men made her faintly uneasy now that she had time to think about it. Boats like this must cost a lot of money, and this one was obviously new. By very token of their being free like this mid-week it appeared that the two of them were, as the saying went, of independent means. Hardly an unusual state of affairs in this part of the world, so why should she suddenly feel that the image didn't quite fit?

It was Marie who put the question for her as Rafe brought the powerful engine to life, voice casual. "If it isn't a rude question, what exactly do you two do for a living?"

Again came that swift exchange of glances, then Rafe laughed, opening the throttle as they cleared the jetty in a roar of sound which almost drowned his reply. "As little as we can, eh, Sven?"

Marie showed no sign of perturbation. "Must be a lot of profit in beachcombing," she observed to no one in particular, and drew a swift grin from Sven as he took a seat alongside.

"Depends what gets washed up. Cigarette?" His eyes moved on to Gina after she accepted the offer. "Do you smoke?"

Gina didn't except on rare occasions, but she refrained from saying so. She accepted a light from the hand he stretched across, feeling the deck vibrating through the thin soles of her sandals as they continued to pick up speed. At present they appeared to be heading straight out to sea. No doubt they would turn to parallel the coast any moment.

"How far along is this beach we're going to?" she asked as one moment passed into another with no change in direction. "We seem to he going a long way out."

"Thirty miles, give or take a couple," Sven agreed without turning a hair. "Friend of ours owns this island. Ideal place for parties—no neighbours to complain about the racket. It's open house to all in the know."

Faint doubt became sudden suspicion, sharp and penetrating. "You said it wasn't far," she accused on a rising note.

"So it isn't. Be there in an hour or so."

He seemed unmoved by her agitation. "Feel like a drink?"

"I want to go back." Her voice had a slight tremor to it. "Marie . . ."

"Marie doesn't want to go back, do you?" Sven was smiling as he looked at the older girl, a glint of mockery in his eyes. "Marie wants to go to the party."

Shapely shoulders lifted in a careless shrug. "May as well now we're on the way. One beach is much the same as another in these parts."

"But we'll no sooner get there than we'll have to set off back again if we're going to make dinner," Gina protested. "It's hardly going to be worthwhile . . ." Her voice petered out before the complete lack of sympathetic response from either party. Nothing she said was going to get through, that was becoming increasingly obvious.

Sven's next words confirmed the impression. "So what if you don't make dinner? You can eat all you want where we're going. Relax, darling. Be like your friend here and enjoy what's going. You'll get back."

When it suits us to bring you back. The words hung unspoken in the air. Gina stared at him helplessly, then glanced beyond him to Rafe at the wheel, but there was no help to be gained there either; she hadn't really expected there would be.

Beside her, Marie smoked her cigarette in apparent unconcern, causing her to wonder if her own reactions were perhaps a shade overwrought. She tried to rationalise her thoughts. All right, so she didn't like these kind of tactics and wished she had had the sense to refuse the invitation in the first place, but that aside, was there really anything to get in a twist over? They might have to reconcile themselves to a rather longer stay than they had bargained for—at least than she had bargained for—but they had to return some time this evening if their absence was not to be noted at the hotel and the alarm raised. Plenty of people had seen them get into the boat and could say in which direction they had been heading, and both Sven and Rafe must realise it. They'd have them back before they were missed.

They'd make sure of that. Not that it excused them anything.

"I don't seem to have much choice," she said wryly. "I just don't like being tricked, that's all."

Sven looked amused. "Would you have come if you'd known where the party was?"

"No, but . . ."

"There you are, then," as though that settled the argument. "Could say we'd done you a favour getting you off the spot for a while. No good coming out here for a good time and then sitting around waiting for it to happen."

"Amen," said Marie with feeling. She got up and went to stand beside Rafe, smiling at him when he glanced at her. "Can I take over for a few minutes?"

"It could cost you." The words were soft, the insinuation not so.

She laughed, slipping in front of him to take the wheel as he made room for her and making no demur when he stayed close behind her with his hands resting lightly on her hips. "I always wanted to drive one of these things. Next best to a good fast car!"

"Better than any car in these parts," said Rafe. "You don't run out of sea."

Gina tried to lighten her mood and join in the banter and general conversation over the next hour, but her heart wasn't in it. She was relieved when the long, low shape of the island for which they were heading finally hove into view. The sooner they were on their way back the better she would feel.

Ringed by apparently unbroken coral heads, at first the island seemed unapproachable. On the leeward side, however, there were gaps through which a boat could penetrate to the smooth green waters beyond. Rafe took the launch in with the confidence of long acquaintance, heading for a wooden jetty jutting into the water's edge to the left of the curving white beach with its backdrop of leaning palms.

Behind it lay a large, single-storey house built of timber and stone and fronted by a covered verandah along the whole length. There were other craft already moored at the jetty and beached along the shoreline, and a number of people on view along the verandah and the portion of beach immediately below the house. Somebody saw them coming in and waved a hand with what looked like a glass held in it. A faint ragged cheer floated across the water, accompanied by a background of music.

"Are we the last comers?" asked Marie lightly, and received a shrug from Rafe as he killed the engine to bring them skilfully alongside the jetty.

"Maybe, maybe not. People come and go as they want."

Stepping from the launch with Sven's help, Gina voiced her question with diffidence, aware of eyes on them from the beach below. "How long is it likely to go on for?"

"Anybody's guess. Last time it was three days. This only started last night."

"Three *days*!" She stopped dead, staring at him in consternation. "You mean these people might still be here at the weekend?"

"Some might, others won't. Like Rafe

51

said, it's open house while it lasts." He slid an arm about her shoulders, tightening his grasp a little when she tensed against it. "Now don't start being unfriendly. Come and have some fun."

She forced herself to move with him along the jetty in the wake of the other two, hating the too close proximity of his body against hers and the possessive weight of that arm along her neck. Short of making a scene right here and now there was little she could do but play along until the moment when she could make her escape from him. If people were coming and going all the time it should surely be possible to find someone else to take her back to New Providence. What Marie did was her own affair.

They were stopped several times in their progress up the beach towards the house, the greetings in most cases heavy with innuendo. Sven countered them in the same vein, not bothering to perform any introductions even of first names. The other two had disappeared among the crowds thronging the verandah by the time they reached it. Gina found a glass pushed into her hand, and took a cautious sniff at the contents before discarding it on to a convenient table.

"I don't like gin," she said.

"Okay, I'll find you a rum and Coke," Sven said amicably. "Just park yourself against the rail and wait for me. The bar's through the back."

A man seated on the floor with his back against the house wall gave her a speculative look as Sven vanished indoors. He was fiftyish, with a flabby, jowled, heavy-featured face and thinning sandy hair. The shirt he was wearing looked crumpled and had perspiration stains under the armpits. From the way he lifted the glass he held towards his lips he had been drinking for some time already.

Gina turned quickly away, hoping he wouldn't attempt to get up and come over to her, her glance roving the press of bodies in search of Marie, though without success. One thing which did strike her was that while the men present at this gathering were of greatly varying age groups, all the females appeared to be young. So far she hadn't seen one girl who looked more than the early twenties.

Only a few yards away, one particularly lovely little redhead who couldn't be more than nineteen stood with arms entwined about the neck of a man almost old enough to be her grandfather, lips pouting provocatively as she gazed into his eyes. She was wearing a short white crocheted dress with the briefest of flesh-coloured pants beneath and nothing else. Even as Gina looked, her companion dropped a fleshy kiss on the inviting upturned mouth, then turned her towards the house with a look on his face that few could mistake for anything but what it was.

Sven came back with her drink, pressing the tall glass into her hand and taking a long pull at his own. He looked flushed and dishevelled, with a smear of lipstick at one corner of his mouth.

"Don't just stand there," he said. "Drink your drink and let your hair down. Your friend Marie is having a good time."

Gina put the glass to her lips obediently

and almost choked on the strong taste of the rum all but obliterating the Coke. "It's too strong," she said. "I can't drink it like this." Despite the heat, she felt a faint shiver run through her as she met the knowing derisive eyes. "Sven, I want to go back," she appealed. "I shouldn't have come. It isn't my scene."

"How do you know till you've tried it?" His tone was without concern. "Come on, honey, you're not that green. What did you come to this part of the world for if it wasn't to live it up?"

"The sun, the scenery—to travel, I suppose." Her voice trailed away.

"Your friend has other ideas."

"Yes, but I didn't realise before we came. You see, I don't know her all that well. We just happen to work in the same office and when I won . . ." She stopped again, wondering why she was bothering to explain her motives to someone so obviously uninterested as this man. "It was a mistake," she finished flatly. "We're different types."

"Maybe not as much as you like to

think." One hand came out to curve her shoulder through the thin material of her jacket, the palm damp. "You're here because you want to be or you wouldn't have come at all. You're a good-looking kid, Gina baby. Not as showy as your friend in there, but I like a bit of reserve." The hand moved up to her chin, forcing up her head and holding it there, his eyes travelling down the taut line of her throat to the curve of her breasts above the blue bikini top. "I can show you a good time —a real good time!"

"Don't!" Jerkily she moved her head away from his fingers. "I don't want your kind of good time, thanks! If you won't take me back, I'll find somebody who will!"

"Want to bet?" He made no attempt to grab her again, leaning against the nearby post with a sneer on his lips. "Go and try if you want. I can wait."

Gina left him standing there, losing the glass en route to the double glass doors which gave access to the house. Inside the huge room immediately opening off the verandah, there were people standing, sitting, even lying about on the pine floor. The furnishings, or what she could see of them through the smoke and press of bodies, were sumptuous, the whole atmosphere reeking of money.

Noise rose about her in waves, an occasional voice standing out above the rest for a moment, as the sound ebbed and flowed. Way over on her left she caught a glimpse of Marie close-wrapped in Rafe's arms, moving to the beat of the music coming from some hidden source in total oblivion to all going on about her. Any appeal in that direction was obviously going to be a complete waste of time. Gina turned her attention back to her immediate surroundings, looking for a friendly face.

But there weren't any—at least, not friendly in the way she wanted them to be. Somebody made a grab for her as she pushed past, putting a heavy arm about her waist and hugging her close.

"Looking for me, honeychild?"

She tore herself free without even glancing round at the man, elbowing somebody else aside in her desire to get away from the spot. There was a burst of laughter behind her and some derisive commiseration for the man she had rejected, but no one came after her.

At last she managed to get across the room and into the comparative quiet of a corridor running off it. On the other side of a wide inner hall, she found a room with a half opened door and no light within, and slipped inside. The room was empty apart from its furnishings, the swiftly vanishing sun lending an eerie red glow to white walls and flimsy curtains. Thankfully she closed the door behind her and sank down on the nearest of the two satin-covered beds, wishing there was a key she could turn in the lock for complete safety.

What she was going to do next she had no idea. From the look of those people out there any appeal for help would meet with little success. The only thing she could do, it appeared, was to stay out of the way until the party showed signs of quieting down, and then look up Marie in the hope that she would be ready and willing to add her insistence towards being taken back to the hotel.

She would have to be eventually. They could hardly spend the night here without being missed when they failed to pick up their key. Yet would anyone really bother if two girls on holiday failed to show up for one night? It probably happened all the time out here—and other places too, for that matter. Her own naïveté had landed her in this situation, nothing else. For the first time in days she allowed herself to think about Ryan Barras and what he had said to her that first night— what he would say to her now if he were here. Idiot, she reflected bitterly. He had been right: she just wasn't equipped for this kind of scene.

Darkness fell with its customary rapidity, bringing its own added complications. Gina made no attempt to switch on any lights, curling up on the bed with her arms about her knees and a fervent wish in her heart for some easy solution to her problems. She supposed she could always try threatening Sven with the police if he didn't immediately take her back, but she had a sneaking suspicion that any such threat might bring little weight to bear in present circumstances. It might even be dangerous to threaten him. No one really knew where they'd been taken.

Eventually, despite herself, she dozed off, wakening with a jerk some time later to the opening of the door and the sudden flood of light from the corridor outside. Sven stood framed in the doorway swaying slightly on his feet as he looked at her startled face. His smile was not a reassuring one.

"So this is where you got to," he said. The words sounded slurred. "Saves time. You and me have some catching up to do, baby."

He closed the door again and lurched towards the bed, his breathing laboured. There was a strong smell of whisky about him, curling Gina's lip in disgust. She slid off the far side of the bed as he made a grab for her, darting round the foot to make for the door before he could recover his balance sufficiently to turn and block her way. His intentions if she stayed here were obvious, and she doubted if anyone would bother lifting a finger to stop him, even if her cries for help could be heard above the racket still going on out there. Where she was going she had no idea and didn't much care. Anywhere, providing it put distance between the two of them.

Somehow she found an outer door and wrenched it open, expecting any moment to feel his hand on her shoulder and smell that horrible whisky smell again. The night air felt blessedly cool against her near-naked skin, dimming the panic a little as she took in great breaths of it.

She had come out at the front of the house facing away from the beach. There were flower beds and a curving, sandy driveway leading out into a narrow lane backed by casuarinas. Beyond those the ground rose in a gentle slope to a belt of vegetation which looked thick enough to hide in. Without stopping to think about it, Gina ran on light, sandalled feet to do just that, driving herself to move faster than she had ever moved in her life before for fear of being seen by someone from the house.

The belt of palms proved thinner than she had first anticipated, giving way to sandy scrubland. Eventually she had to stop for breath, listening between pants for sounds of pursuit and with relief hearing none.

Only then, sinking down beside a convenient bush, did she start to wonder just where she went from here. No way was she going back to that house tonight, and yet what else was there? For all she knew, nobody else lived on the island, but the owner she had not even met. No neighbours to complain about the racket, she remembered Sven saying. That seemed to clinch it. She was on her own against the lot of them down there.

Finally she decided the only possible course was to wait for morning, by which time even Marie might be prepared to make a stand against being kept here any longer. At any rate, by daylight surely someone would be sobered up enough to listen to an appeal for help in getting back to New Providence.

She dozed through the night in fits and starts, aware of a growing heaviness in the air every time she woke. First light brought a brassy look to the sky soon dispelled by the rising sun, although a faint haze still clung to the horizon.

It was very still, the trees motionless, the heat already lifting shimmering veils from the white sand. From where she was she could see the house spread out below and slightly to the right of her. A few bodies were stretched out on the beach adjoining, but there was no sign of movement either there or anywhere within the building.

After a moment or two she began to move cautiously down towards the beach, not yet quite sure what she was going to do when she got there. After a night sleeping out she felt both stiff and dirty and would have given anything for a wash, except that it meant going into the house for that and she didn't want to run the risk of meeting up with Sven again before she found Marie.

Some of the boats had gone from their moorings, she noted, but the launch was still riding there at the end of the jetty. The sight of it gave rise to an idea which at first seemed ludicrous but which gradually took on stronger and stronger appeal. Watching Rafe at the controls yesterday, she had thought how easy it looked to handle. Certainly Marie seemed to have found little difficulty in doing so. Bringing the engine to life was simply a matter of turning an ignition switch, much as one started a car. And she knew where the throttle was too. They had steered almost due north on the way out, so if she took the opposite compass point she could hardly go far wrong, she told herself with the easy confidence of total ignorance. There were other things to be considered, of course. Like Marie, for instance. Gina did so briefly, then deliberately hardened her heart. Marie deserved to be stranded here along with the men. It might teach her a lesson. They could all of them hitch a lift back with someone else when they were ready. By that time she would be safely back in the hotel where no one could touch her. Any attempt to do so and all she had to do was threaten to go to the police about her enforced stay here on this island. That should settle the matter.

Nobody attempted to stop her on her way to the jetty for the simple reason that nobody appeared to be awake. Apparently even parties of this kind had to have the occasional natural break. She unhitched the mooring rope from the post, and then had to practically dive head-first into the cockpit as the launch immediately began drifting out. By the time she had righted herself and gathered her wits, they were already several yards from the jetty with the bows coming round slowly of their own accord towards the open sea.

The ignition fired first time, the noise shattering on the still morning air. Gina glanced shorewards in trepidation, but nobody appeared to have heard anything, or if they had were studiously ignoring it.

Cautiously she opened the throttle a

little way and felt an immediate surge of power beneath her. She brought the bows all the way round and pointed them in the direction of the largest gap in the reef, stilling a sudden sense of panic at the memory of Rafe's careful steering coming through. She could do it provided she kept her head. All she had to do was steer in a straight line, and in water as calm as this that should be no problem.

What she had not allowed for was the current running within the gap itself where the sheltered waters met the open sea, and it almost proved her undoing. It was sheer luck which caused her to spin the wheel in the right direction, because she had no idea what she was doing. A spur of coral scraped along the keel as the stern swung sharply across, but she was through and safe, meeting the unpleasantly choppy little waves with a motion which did her stomach no good at all.

Something nasty was brewing; that was fast becoming apparent from the hazed look of the sky and the build-up of cloud on the horizon. Not to worry, she reassured herself, she would be home and dry long before the storm hit. She set the boat on a due south heading, a little disconcerted to find that it took considerable effort of concentration to keep the helm even reasonably steady against the pull of tide and current. For the first time it occurred to her that New Providence wasn't all that big an island itself. Supposing she missed it? But of course she wouldn't. Maybe she might not make landfall at exactly the same beach from which they had set sail the previous afternoon, but wherever she landed she could easily find her way back—although dressed the way she was that might prove embarrassing. Still, she would face that particular problem when she came to it. For the present her sole aim had to be in reaching land at all.

Long before the storm hit she had begun to acknowledge that handling a boat this size was not the child's play she had imagined. She only had to take her eyes off the compass for a moment or two to find the boat had veered wildly from its course. Somewhere she had read about weather vanes which could be connected to the helm to steer an automatic course, but even if this boat possessed one she would have no idea how to use it, she acknowledged fatalistically.

The sky was heavy now and brooding, the sea risen to a height which frightened her more than a little. When the rain came it did so with a ferocity that left her gasping for breath, soaking her to the skin in seconds. Half blinded, she felt the wheel slip from her grasp and spin, and was thrown off balance by the wild swing of the bows, finishing up on her knees in the cockpit well with panic welling inside her. Given good weather all the way, she might eventually have made New Providence, but in this she stood no chance at all. It had been an idiotic gesture from the start, she realised. Knowing as little about boats and navigation as she did, even as short a distance as thirty miles became tantamount to crossing the Atlantic.

Somehow she managed to crawl across and kill the engine, then found a life jacket in one of the seat lockers and struggled into it. The cabin would have afforded protection from the elements, but she dared not run the risk of being caught inside should the boat capsize. Instead she huddled down in the lee of the superstructure. It was in the laps of the gods whether she came through this or not. Cold, wet and sick, at this precise moment she hardly cared any more.

How many hours passed before the rain finally began to let up, Gina had no way of knowing. It seemed like days. She had been sick time and time again, kneeling on the bare boards in racking agony and a fervent desire to die.

Carried by wind and waves, the boat rolled and wallowed like a dead log, a lone craft in all that expanse of water. By now she could be anywhere, heading in any direction. And the storm was by no means over; she had a horrible feeling it was only just beginning. The sky was as black as pitch shot through with queerly hued lights, the air full of sound. It was like being in hell, except that no hell could be as wet as this.

The sounds became louder, taking on a recognisable quality which brought her head straining upwards above the bulwarks. Those were breakers up ahead, which meant a reef jutting above the surface of the sea—and a reef meant land in the vicinity. At least she hoped it did.

And there it was, only dimly glimpsed through the tossing white spray but real enough to bring a small cry of thankfulness to her lips. The relief lasted only seconds before realisation hit her. The island she had left had been almost completely surrounded by coral heads, and so probably was this one too. If the boat hit those razor-sharp teeth it would break up under her within minutes; it needed no seamanship to know that. Struggling to her feet, she pulled herself across to the helm and reached for the ignition. With power she might stand a chance of pulling away.

It was too late, of course. It had been too late from the moment she had recognised the sound of breaking water. The boat hit even as her fingers found the switch, sliding across the top of the reef with a sound like ripping cloth and a horrible lurching motion which sent her tumbling once more to the deck.

Clinging to the metal rod holding the fire extinguisher in place, Gina waited with bated breath and a dreadful fear in her heart for the moment when the water rushing in through the ripped hull would send her plummeting to the bottom, but nothing happened except that the boat kept on moving, carried onwards by the very wave which had lifted it across a low section of reef until it finally met the shore proper with an impetus that carried it half its length out of the water.

Wasting no time in thanking providence for her deliverance, Gina hoisted herself over the side into knee-deep waves and stumbled ashore. The rain was still coming down hard enough to sting her skin, numbed though it was, but at least she was on solid land again and in one piece. That this was not New Providence she needed no telling. From what she had seen from the sea it was little more than an islet rising to a low prominence in the middle. But whatever, it represented safety, and that was all she wanted for the moment. Safety, and perhaps a little shelter from the elements once she felt able to make the effort to find some.

The sight of the figure coming through the trees backing the beach made her believe at first that she was seeing things. She tried to get to her feet, but the wind pressed her down again, tearing at the flimsy jacket and whipping her hair over her eyes.

Still struggling, she felt hands seize and lift her, and the hardness of a male body beneath the wet oilskins as she was swung up in a pair of strong arms. The face beneath the sou'wester came as a shock so complete it drove the last ounce of breath from her leaving her limp and mute as she gazed into familiar grey eyes. Then, for the first time in her life, she fainted.

# 3

SHE regained consciousness to find herself lying on the beach, and for a moment believed she really had been dreaming. Then Ryan came back, kneeling in the wet sand at her side to lift her again.

"Sorry I had to leave you," he said, lifting his voice above the elements. "Had to make sure there was nobody else in the cabin."

She closed her eyes as he began carrying her up the beach, still unable to wholly trust her senses. What was Ryan Barras doing here on this island? It didn't make sense!

"The boat," she stammered. "It isn't mine!"

"It's pretty well beached," he said. "And from the look of the bottom it's going to stay that way for some time. Quit

73

worrying about it. You're lucky you made it to land without foundering."

"I got caught in the storm," she whispered, and saw him bend his head closer to catch the words. "Caught in the storm!"

"Obviously. You almost got yourself killed in it too." He looked down at her, face grim beneath the streaking wet. "Just keep quiet till we get inside, then we can talk."

The oilskins scarcely made an ideal resting place, but she felt incapable of walking. She felt so totally unreal. Yet there was no doubting the reality of the arms supporting her weight, nor the discomfort of cold wetness on her body. The life jacket had gone, presumably removed by Ryan before she came round.

The house lay some distance from the beach, sheltered by a windbreak of trees. Without altering his grasp, Ryan mounted the steps to a verandah and kicked open a door to stride inside, greeting the young Alsatian dog which came padding towards them with a single word of command.

"Pal won't hurt you," he said, setting Gina back on her feet but keeping a supporting arm about her waist as the dog sniffed curiously at her. "First thing you need is a hot bath and then some dry clothes. Questions later. All right?"

She nodded, scarcely trusting her voice. Her knees felt like jelly and she was trembling right through. Shock, she realised. It had to come, of course. One couldn't go through the kind of experience she had come through without some reaction.

She allowed herself to be led towards another door on the far side of the room, through a hallway and into a small but adequately equipped bathroom tiled in yellow and white. Ryan left her standing in the middle of the floor while he went over to turn on both taps to full, releasing a jet of steam into the room.

"Good thing I ran the generator long enough to heat the tank again," he said. "Must have known you were coming."

He turned when she made no answer, eyeing her slender, trembling form for a brief impassive moment before straightening. "I'll go and find you something to wear."

Gina made an effort to pull herself together as he went out. What Ryan Barras was doing here on this island in this house and apparently alone, she could only guess. He had said he needed solitude to write. This must be it. It was the sheer unbelievable coincidence of landing up here herself which took her breath away. His too, if she was any judge. Back there on the beach when he had picked her up he had looked totally shattered. She was going to have a lot of explaining to do, that was for sure, and the thought dismayed her. How could she admit to being the kind of fool she had been?

She was lying in the hot water and luxuriating in the return of feeling to her lower extremities when the door opened again without warning. Sitting hastily upright, she made an involuntary movement to cover herself with an arm across her breasts, staring at him with widened eyes.

"They're going to be a bit on the large side," he said, tossing a couple of garments over the cane chair in the corner, "but it's the best I can do." He looked directly at her then, a faint, cynical smile flicking the corners of his mouth as he registered her frozen demeanour. "It's all right, I've seen naked women before—and with rather more to hide than you've got. Rub yourself well down when you get out and get your circulation gingered up again. I'll be seeing to some food."

It was a moment or two before Gina could bring herself to relax a muscle after he had gone out again. Her face burned. He had done that deliberately, as if to underline the fact that his gallantry only went so far. She wondered how he would react to the knowledge that his advice had gone unheeded—if he hadn't already worked that much out for himself.

The shirt and shorts he had provided needed a great deal of tucking and tying before they would consent to stay secured. There was nothing for her feet, and her own sandals were sodden rags of leather and canvas. After rinsing through her bikini and wrap in clean water, she wrung them out and hung them over the towel rail to dry before going in search of her host, steeling herself for the moment of confrontation.

She found him in the act of carrying through a tray containing a couple of steaming dishes from what appeared to be the kitchen, and at his invitation followed him back into the square, multi-purpose living room. The floor was sanded wood scattered with rugs, the furnishings comfortable without being in any way ostentatious. A fire burned brightly in the big stone fireplace, lending a cheery glow to the storm-darkened room. There was no sign of the dog.

Ryan placed the tray on a convenient table close by the fireplace and indicated a chair. "Sit down and have something to eat. It's not really cold enough for a fire, but it lends a certain comfort at a time like this, don't you think?" It was a rhetorical question. "Feeling better?"

Gina took the chair and held out her

hands to the flames in a gesture born purely of nerves. "I was," she said pointedly. "Where I came from people don't walk into an occupied bathroom without invitation."

His shrug held no apology. "What would you have preferred, your things on the floor? In case you hadn't noticed, it was damp."

"Anyway, it's your house and you'll do as you think fit," she came back, determined not to be put on the defensive.

"If that's how you want to see it." He handed her a bowl of thick meaty stew. "Get that down you and tell me what you were doing on that boat on your own."

She looked from him to the stew and back again. "At the same time?"

"We're not standing on any ceremony. Just get on with it."

She had already considered concocting some story which would cover the salient points without revealing her in such a bad light, but honesty refused to allow her to take that way out. Pride took over now.

Let him have the truth. Why should she care what he thought of her?

He listened without comment while she told him the whole story from the moment of meeting Sven and Rafe on the beach, features revealing neither censure no sympathy at any time. Only when she had finished and her voice had trailed away into silence did he pronounce any judgment.

"You're either the greenest female I ever met." he said evenly, "or the biggest liar. I can't decide which."

She flared. "I'm no liar!"

"Then we'll settle for the other. Obviously you didn't listen to a word I said the other night."

"I listened," she said. "I didn't have much choice. This situation was . . . different."

"How?"

"Well, I thought they were just being friendly at first."

"So you blithely take off into the wide blue yonder with a couple of guys you've never seen before and know damn-all about. Personally I'd say you asked for all you got—and more!"

"Thanks." Her tone was frigid. "Being a man, you'd naturally appreciate their point of view!"

"That women are just around for amusement?" He shook his head. "Depends on the woman. Kids like you are rare enough to be unrecognisable round these parts. I guess those two might have had some excuse for taking you at face value when you agreed to go with them in the first place."

Gina set down her empty dish with what dignity she could muster. "I'm twenty-three. That makes me rather more than a kid!"

"I wasn't speaking in years. Some never mature. Still, I imagine this experience must have taught you something."

"Oh, I'm learning all the time," she came back bitterly. "I even got kissed by a famous author the other night. Purely out of kindness, of course!"

He studied her with deliberation, eyes sliding the length of her body down to her slim bare legs and feet and back again to her face via the same route. "We could try it again," he said. "I never made love to a sea urchin before."

She made herself return his gaze without flinching. "I doubt if I could provide you with the kind of material you'd be likely to find useful. And don't debase the word love either. It doesn't mean what you're talking about."

"Is that right?" His tone was derisive. "And what would you call what I'm talking about?"

"Dissoluteness," she retorted promptly and scornfully. "Your affairs are common knowledge, Mr. Barras. One of America's leading models last time I heard. Or is she old news now?"

The grey eyes had narrowed. He said softly, "You've no sense of discretion at all, have you? Did it occur to you that we're on our own here?"

Her heart missed a beat, then steadied again. "Are you threatening me?" she asked with remarkable calmness.

"I'm not sure. Keep up that line and we might find out."

"I'd have thought you'd be used to it by now."

"Not from little girls who don't know what they're talking about."

"Oh, I'm old enough to know what goes on between men and women. Especially after reading your books. Your bedroom scenes are very explicit." She was too angry to care what she was saying. "I suppose the graphic sex is there to sell the book. It usually is. You might lose too large a portion of your market if you left it out!"

He was looking at her as if he hadn't really seen her properly until this moment, an expression on his face she found hard to decipher. "Tell me more," he said as she paused. "This is getting interesting."

She went suddenly flat. "There isn't any more. I've said all I want to say."

"I don't think so, Let's have the rest."

It took her a moment to marshal her forces again, but if he wanted it he should have it. She was sick of him, sick of this whole horrible holiday. She had wasted a thousand pounds on coming here, and everything had gone wrong.

"All right," she said thickly. "I *despise* people like you! People who think they can do exactly as they think fit because they happen to be in a so-called superior position. I do things because I don't stop to think long enough, *you* know exactly what you're doing and why. If you felt like playing the kindly counsellor the other night you could have done just that, but you had to underline it the way you did. It wasn't necessary. You just enjoyed putting me in my place—as you no doubt called it!"

There was tension in the line of his jaw. "What would *you* consider your place?" he asked very quietly.

"Wherever *I* want it to be."

"That's good." He came slowly to his feet, lean and muscular in the slim-fitting jeans and tee-shirt, a latent power in the breadth of his shoulders. His face was expressionless. "Have you had enough to eat?"

The quick change of subject disconcerted her. She stared at him, only just beginning to appreciate how far she had gone. What she had said was true in part, but there had been no need for quite that amount of quivering invective in her voice. If he had come across and hit her she wouldn't have been all that surprised, but this total disregard was outside her understanding.

"Yes," she said at last. "Yes, thanks."

"Then I'll go and bring the dog through."

He took the tray and dishes with him, leaving her sitting there in wry acknowledgement of having been put more thoroughly in her place than any words could have achieved. She wasn't even worth the trouble of slapping down, metaphorically or otherwise. At this moment she could almost appreciate his feelings. He hadn't asked to be landed with her, but he had extended his help and hospitality. To have the recipient of his efforts turn on him the way she had just done must fill him with disgust. Well, it was too late to apologise. She doubted if he would bother listening anyway. She had set the mood, and must bear with it now for the duration of her stay.

There would be no getting away tonight, she reflected unhappily, listening to the rain lashing against the windows. The wind was stronger than ever, coming in gusts which sounded wild. It was difficult to believe that this was the same hemisphere which only twenty-four hours ago had basked in hot sunshine under a clear blue sky. The change was appalling.

Ryan returned with the Alsatian padding at his side. The latter gave Gina a long hard glance but made no attempt to come to her, lying down in front of the fire with his eyes fixed on the tall figure of his master.

"He'll get used to having you around," said Ryan. "He's going to have to."

"How long do you think it will be before I can get back to the mainland?" she asked in a subdued voice.

"Depends on the weather," he said. "That wind out there isn't going to drop for some time, and while that blows the sea stays too rough to launch a boat. I guess we're stuck with each other for at least another twenty-four hours, if not longer."

Dismay clouded her eyes. "I've already been gone from the hotel more than twenty-four hours. Can't you at least inform them I'm here?"

"How? I don't run a transmitter, and they didn't get round to laying underwater cables in this direction yet."

She flushed. "There's no need to be so sarcastic!"

"There is if you think this place is some kind of off-shore resort. We're twenty-five miles north-east of Nassau and on our own till this blows over. The sooner you accept that as fact the better."

"North-*east*!" Gina knew enough to realise what that meant. If she hadn't fetched up on this tiny island she could easily have been swept right out into the Atlantic, with no one any the wiser for her disappearance. For the first time it occurred to her to wonder what had happened to Marie and the others. No doubt they were still safely ashore waiting for the storm to finish before making an attempt to return to Nassau. Which meant two of them missing from the hotel.

"Won't the police be called in when we don't get back to the hotel after a couple of days?" she asked worriedly. "Surely . . ."

"Maybe after three or four they might start thinking along those lines." He shrugged at her expression. "This isn't England. It's unlikely they'll worry too much about whether you're occupying your room or not. The one sure time you're likely to be missed is when you're due to check out."

"That isn't for another fifteen days!"

"Well, you should be home and dry long before then."

"How?" The thought had only just occurred to her.

"I didn't see any other boat down there on the beach."

"Perhaps because I happen to moor it in the lagoon."

His tone was short. "Take my word for

it, I'll have you out of here the minute the weather allows for it. Till then you're just going to have to grin and bear it. And don't concern yourself—there's another bed apart from mine."

Gina bit her lip. If it was going to be like this the whole time life would become unbearable. She said impulsively, "I'm sorry for what I said just now. I was upset, I spoke off the top."

He eyed her for a long, speculative moment before lifting his shoulders. "Forget it."

"I will if you will."

Something flickered for a second in the grey eyes. "I already have."

She had to accept that, yet deep down she felt a momentary doubt. Was he really that indifferent, or did that very lack of expression indicate a rigid control over his true feelings? She would rather have faced anger than this peculiar uncertainty.

"How about a drink?" he said. "I can't offer you a vast selection, but there's some Bacardi, I think."

She hesitated. "Would you mind if I made myself some coffee instead?"

"Not a bit. I'll show you where everything is, then you can help yourself whenever you feel like it."

He took her through to the kitchen, leaving Pal guarding the fire. Like the bathroom, it was small but well thought out, with a Calor gas stove to cook on, plus the essential refrigerator.

"I can't hear the generator," Gina remarked as he switched on an overhead light. "I always thought they were very noisy."

"They can be. This one is housed some distance away in a specially sound-proofed enclosure. I don't need that kind of distraction."

"Did you have the house built yourself?"

"No, I took it over as it stood from the previous owner. It used to be a weekend retreat."

He showed her where things were and how to light the stove, then went back to the living room to see to his own preference, telling her to come on through when she was ready.

Waiting for the kettle to boil, Gina tried to come to terms with her situation. For the time being she was marooned here and must accept it, yet she couldn't stop worrying about what was going to happen when she did get back. She could hear the sound of the sea out there, and wondered how the boat she had wrecked was faring. There was going to be trouble over the damage, although no doubt it was insured. Anyway, she told herself stoutly, those two had asked for it. Perhaps in future they'd be more careful about who they picked on to share their idea of entertainment.

Ryan was sitting in lamplight with a glass of what looked like whisky in his hand when she got back to the living room. She was surprised to see her sodden sandals laid out on the hearthstone close by the glowing logs.

"They wouldn't have dried very fast in the bathroom," he commented dryly, following her glance. "That's one department I can't help you in at all, I'm afraid. I take a size nine."

"Beggars can't be choosers," Gina agreed with a wry glance down at herself. "It's a good thing you're not enormous round the hips or I'd never keep these on." She looked up then and caught his glance, and felt the colour faintly tinge her cheeks. "Have you any idea at all how long this thing might go on for?" she asked hurriedly. "You must have experienced seasonal storms like this before."

"I have, but they're unpredictable. Even when the wind dies down the sea can stay rough for some time, and I'm not an expert enough sailor to risk the reef in anything but good weather. Normally I go over to Nassau once a week for supplies, but I can live off tinned goods for quite a time if necessary."

"What would happen if you were taken ill or had an accident?" she ventured. "I mean, with no way of contacting anyone you could. . . ."

"Die?" he finished for her. He sounded unmoved by the possibility. "If I didn't keep my regular rendezvous with Neil he'd know something was wrong and come out to investigate."

"Radio would be simpler."

"Not necessarily. If I were lying unconscious somewhere I could no more use a radio than I could sail a boat. And I prefer a sense of isolation when I'm working. It gives me inspiration just to know I'm not going to be interrupted."

Gina said uncomfortably, "I'll try and stay out of your way as much as possible while I'm here."

"It isn't too important now. I've finished, all but the tightening up."

"Oh?" She was immediately interested. "Can I ask what this one is about?"

"No," he said, not unpleasantly. "I hate dissecting a book orally. The written word has a different feel to it." He studied her, expression enigmatic in the soft light from the lamps, dark hair falling in a thick comma across his forehead. "Writers are a breed all on their own, you know. Like artists or musicians—we all have our quirks." The pause was barely perceptible, his tone subtly altering. "You look ready for bed."

She glanced at him swiftly, but there was an alteration to his expression. She was reading innuendo where it didn't exist, she decided.

"I do feel a bit shattered," she confessed. "It seems a month since this morning."

"And you couldn't have had much sleep last night either." He put down his glass and got to his feet. "I'll go and see about some bedding for the spare room. Finish your coffee."

Her eyes followed him as he went out, a small frown drawn between her brows. On the surface he appeared perfectly natural and easy, yet something bothered her about him. Imagination on her part perhaps, because of what she had said to him earlier. Why couldn't she accept that she hadn't even reached him, that he didn't give a damn what she thought? He was being friendly now because there was no point in being anything else when they were going to be stuck with one another for some time.

It took a low growl from the direction of the hearth to remind her she was not alone. Pal had lifted his head and was gazing at her fixedly, the beautiful amber eyes glinting with a light which set her heart thudding in sudden quick fear. She conquered the latter emotion with an effort, returning the animal's gaze steadily as she spoke softly to him.

"All right, Pal, all right, boy! I'm not going to do anything to upset you—or that master of yours. I know I'm an intruder, but I couldn't help it and I'll be gone as soon as possible."

Amazingly the tawny tail gave a sudden thump on the floor and a pink tongue lolled momentarily from the powerful jaws. Instead of a growl, this time there came another sound, halfway between a whine and a whimper, then he was getting to his feet and padding over to push a cold nose into the palm of her hand.

"Why, you're just an old softy, aren't you," smiled Gina, fondling the fine head.

"And to think I was scared of you for a minute!"

"Didn't hold out long, did you, Pal?" came the sardonic comment from the doorway.

"How long have you had him?" Gina asked as Ryan came back across to them. "He can't be very old."

"He's two. I was given him as a pup two books back."

"Surely you don't leave him here when you go away?"

"Not on the island. Neil takes him for me."

"Doesn't he miss you?"

"Naturally. I can hardly take him with me. Many places I go have quarantine restrictions." He was watching the two of them with the twist still there at the corner of his mouth, the latter increasing a fraction when the dog left Gina to come to him. "Still know which side your bread's buttered on, don't you, boy?"

"I suppose you'd find life very lonely here without him," Gina commented, and drew a faint smile.

"He's the ideal companion six days of the week. If I could teach him to do the chores I'd want for nothing."

Her glance went round the comfortable room. "You keep the place very tidy."

"Considering my bachelor status?" he came back dryly. "You might change your mind when you see it in sunlight. I'm not here to do housework." He watched her try to stifle a yawn and added, "I put the bedding on the bed ready for you to make up yourself. Think you'll be warm enough with just the one blanket?"

She laughed. "You might consider this the cooler part of the year, but to me it's like an oven!" She took the hint, pressing herself upright. "Which is my room?"

"I'll show you."

Both bedrooms were at the back and next to one another. Hers contained a single bed, a dressing table fitment and a deep fitted closet which was no use to her at present. There was a thick-piled rug covering most of the floor, and a reed blind at the window.

"You'll find the bed comfortable

97

enough," Ryan said from the doorway. "I alternate to keep the mattresses aired." His grin was unexpected. "Things my mother taught me. The humidity is a constant problem round here. Are you sure you're feeling okay now? That was quite an experience you went through."

"I'm fine," she assured him. "No after-effects that a good night's sleep won't put right." She hesitated, vitally aware of his presence there in the doorway. "I'm sorry to be such a nuisance."

"I'll put it all on the bill." He remained where he was for a brief moment looking at her, then said softly, "Have a good night, honey."

She stood gazing at the closed door for some time after he had gone. She had always disliked that particular American-ism, yet coming from Ryan it had sounded so different. It didn't mean anything, of course; he probably used it often to a woman, but the fact that he had used it to her seemed to prove that he bore her no grudge for what had passed between them earlier. Perhaps she was wrong in more ways than one about Ryan Barras. The man she had described would not have turned the other cheek.

Despite her weariness, she lay awake for some time listening for the sounds of movement in the house, although the wind and the rain made it difficult to hear anything else. The storm no longer worried her. Deep down inside her she was almost grateful to it for landing her here like this.

# 4

THE rain had stopped by morning, but the sky was still overcast with heavy cloud, trapping the heat and moisture together so that perspiration sprang the moment one was dried off from a shower.

The smell of frying ham tantalised Gina's nostrils when she finally emerged from the bathroom, almost falling over Pal who was lying in the doorway. Ryan was in the kitchen, dressed this morning in a skin-tight white cotton shirt and white drill shorts. His legs, she noted, were strong and well shaped and as bronzed as the rest of him under their fine coating of dark hair. He looked superbly fit. There wasn't a spare ounce of flesh on all that muscular frame.

"Want some ham and eggs?" he asked without glancing round from the stove.

"Please." Gina hadn't realised how

hungry she was until that moment. She hesitated before adding diffidently, "Is there anything I can do?"

"Nothing. I prefer doing it myself." His tone was easy enough, but he obviously meant what he said. "Doesn't look as if we're going to get you away today. There's a big swell still running."

"I know," she said, trying to infuse the right amount of despondency into her voice. "I really am sorry about this mess."

"I'm not complaining." He looked at her then, a smile warming his lips as he took in her appearance. "The sun's been at your hair since I first saw you. Is that its natural colour?"

"Of course."

"There's no of course about it. Hair colour can change overnight. A man could go to bed with a brunette and wake up with a raving redhead!"

Gina laughed. "Has that happened to you?"

"No. But that's because I prefer blondes." He said it easily without de-liberation, his glance holding no trace of mockery. "Though you're the first one I've met who can still look as good first thing in the morning."

She was pleased, flattered but just a little bit wary. "Well . . . thanks."

"You don't care for compliments? That's unusual too. Your sandals are dry if you want to go and fetch them."

She was becoming accustomed to his way of changing the subject at short notice. She went to do so, unable to deny the glow of wellbeing his comments had brought her. Whether he meant it or not it was still nice to hear—and he seemed genuine about it.

"You know," she said softly to Pal who had followed her, "I could finish up falling for your master if I'm not careful." She bent down and rubbed behind the pricked ears, seeing the amber eyes glaze with ecstatic pleasure and knowing just how the animal felt, Ryan could gain something of the same reaction from her with just a glance, much less a caress. She wondered what it would feel like to have him kiss her and mean it, not like the other night when he had wanted only to teach her a lesson. Thinking about that now, she supposed she really had asked for it. Her whole attitude had been provocative of anger. She had even tried to slap him—and been warned that he might hit back. He had been trying to offer good advice because he recognised her inexperience, whereas another man might very well have taken real advantage of it. If she found the right moment she would apologise for that too.

They ate in the living room, seated at a table which pulled up from the wall. In the morning light she could see the dust, and resolved to give the place a quick flick round before she left. Not that he would probably even notice unless he actually saw her doing it. A man could apparently ignore such irrelevant details. She had to concede he had a point. He needed to concentrate entirely on his work, not spend half the day doing things which would only need doing all over again the following day.

"Are you going to work this morning?" she asked when they were almost finished.

"After I've been down to look at that boat of yours, he said. "And my own, of course. It should be okay where it is, but you never know. Any damage to that and it could be days before somebody comes to rescue us, Neil isn't due back till the end of the week."

"I know," she said absently. "Marie told me." She caught the quality in his silence and looked up, face warming a little. "You were right, she was looking for somebody like Neil. I suppose he's very rich."

"Enough."

"Is he married?"

"A widower. Has been for ten years." The pause was brief but telling. "I doubt if he'll marry again now."

And for certain not someone like Marie, Gina acknowledged. But then the other girl, by her own declaration, was willing to settle for less. Well, Neil Davids was old enough to decide for himself, and probably would.

"Tell me about yourself," Ryan said

unexpectedly, pouring them both more coffee. "What do you do for a living?"

"I work for a public relations firm." Gina smiled a little wryly at the slow quirk of one dark eyebrow, knowing she deserved it. "No, just on the secretarial side. As a matter of fact, it's the same firm that handles your personal publicity."

"Small world." He sounded unsurprised. "So that's how you came to recognise me so easily. I don't have such a well known face. How come you have to borrow my books from a library?"

"I've only been there a few months. I was able to get a copy of your last one, but that was all."

"Do you like the work?"

"It's interesting. Something different every day. We've been handling a campaign for the Milk Marketing Board this last couple of months."

"From the sublime to the ridiculous." He studied her a moment, the grey eyes hard to read. "I shouldn't have thought your salary ran to holidays in the Bahamas on any basis."

"It doesn't. A Premium Bond came up."

"And Marie? How did you get mixed up with her?"

"She works for the same firm."

"A higher paid job than yours, apparently."

"Well, yes, but she's been saving for this for a long time."

"With one idea in mind. Her judgment was sound enough. Nassau is the place to be for a woman with her looks and outlook. I still don't understand how you came to be with her."

"She needed a foil, she said—although she didn't call it that until we were on the plane."

"I see." From his tone it was obvious that he saw perfectly. "And you saw Nassau as the one place you had to visit on your winnings?"

"It sounded excitingly far away." Her tone was slightly defensive. "I suppose you think I should have salted it away against a rainy day."

"I didn't say that. Rainy days can take

care of themselves usually. I think you could have chosen a little more wisely, that's all."

"I know, and I agree with you." But she wouldn't have had this, Gina thought. Looking at him across the narrow table, she knew she was building up heartache for herself. They had been thrown together by fortune; he could have no real interest in her. His type of woman was sophisticated and knowledgeable, able to hold her own in the kind of world in which he moved.

"Discretion the better part of valour?" The words were soft, his expression holding something indecipherable. "What happened to last night's little virago?"

She bit her lip. "I told you I was sorry about that."

"So you did." The pause was brief. "Do you still think my love scenes too explicit?"

This time she was unable to control the flush. "I don't suppose so."

His brows had lifted. "Didn't you ever go to bed with a man at all?"

Her stomach muscles knotted suddenly and sharply. "Is that really any of your business?"

"No, but it's interesting. I don't think I ever met a twenty-three-year-old virgin before."

Gina pushed back her chair, scraping the bare boards with a sound which set her teeth on edge. "You don't move in the right circles."

"I'll go along with that." His smiled held cynicism. "Don't get on your high horse. I wasn't criticising. You were right about the sex, it is put in to sell the book. Most of it, at any rate. Today's public demands graphic illustration."

"And you give them what they want."

"That's exactly right. Among the large majority there's a small minority who will appreciate what I'm trying to get across regardless of how many times the hero has a woman on the side. The other night I thought I'd found one of them."

"You did." Her anger had flown. "If there was no deeper theme I'd never have gone on reading them in the first place.

You're a good writer, Ryan—even a great one at times."

"Thanks." There was a certain tilt to his lips. He put down his coffee cup and got to his feet. "I'd better go and check on those boats. Seeing I cooked the breakfast, I'll let you do the clearing up."

He left the house a few minutes later accompanied by Pal. Gina took the plates and mugs through to the kitchen and ran hot water into the bowl, then left them to soak while she went to straighten her bed.

Her face in the dressing mirror looked faintly flushed, her eyes vivid against the tan. Ryan had put that look there, along with the growing yearning inside her. If only things could be different—if only she could be different! She had never met anyone like Ryan before and probably never would again. The thought made her feel so totally disconsolate. How could she go back to living her so desperately ordinary little life after all that had happened to her out here? She had been happy enough in her ignorance. Why couldn't she have stayed where she was?

Ryan's bed was already made, the bedroom neat and tidy. There were no personal items lying around, no photographs on his locker. The only thing which might provide any sort of clue to his personality was the book lying on the bedside table. She went over and picked it up, pausing as an envelope which apparently was in use as a bookmark fluttered to the floor.

The address was a Nassau post box. It was written in a flowing, unmistakably feminine hand. There was no letter inside. She felt guilty over even looking, but the temptation was too much for her. She tried to convince herself that she would not have been tempted to read any letter it might have still contained, but knew it would have been a fight. Where Ryan was concerned all her better instincts seemed to vanish.

He returned some twenty minutes later, coming into the kitchen where she was still putting things away.

"The sky is starting to clear," he

announced. "With any luck the sea will have dropped by tonight."

"Then I might get back today after all?" she said.

"Not a chance. It will be nightfall before conditions improve to that extent." He eyed her for a moment before saying evenly, "Have you thought about what's going to happen when you do get back?"

"About the boat, you mean?"

"For one thing. It will have to be reported."

"But you think I'd be a fool to try fling an official complaint against its owners," she hazarded shrewdly.

"I think you'd be wasting your time, yes. You went aboard willingly. There was no coercion. The authorities would take the view that you were old enough to know what you were doing." He paused. "Stealing and smashing up a valuable boat is another matter."

"So is attempted rape."

"Show me your bruises," he countered, and inclined his head at the look on her face. "I'm only trying to show you the way

111

things are liable to go. Is Marie likely to back you up?"

"I doubt it." Her tone was bitter. "It just isn't fair!"

"That's life." He used the cliché with cynical deliberation. "I'll do what I can."

Gina glanced at him swiftly. "Are you well in with the authorities?"

"I have my contacts—Neil has more. If you'll pass me that old towel from behind the door I'll give Pal a rub down before I bring him in. He got soaked running through wet undergrowth."

She went out to the verandah with him, looking out on a slowly brightening world while he worked on the dog. The flowering bushes growing in profusion about the house were battered by wind and rain, and there were one or two palm fronds lying around, but little sign of any lasting damage anywhere. From this angle there were only glimpses of the sea between the trees, but enough to show how high it still was out beyond the reef. The humidity was oppressive.

"How big is the island?" she asked without turning her head.

"About one by one and a half," said Ryan.

"And there's just this one house?"

"That's right. The previous owners liked solitude too—though for different reasons."

"You mean you own the whole island?"

"That's right," he said again. Having finished wiping the dog, he came to stand at the rail by her side, close but not touching. Taking out a gold cigarette case he offered it to her. "Like one?"

Gina accepted, bending her head to the flame of his lighter. The latter was gold too, she noted. It looked solid. The fingers grasping it had a tensile strength that sent a quiver the length of her spine. She had felt the touch of those hands on her skin, the hardness of that lean body close to hers. She was conscious of him with every fibre, barely able to control the unsteadiness of her own hand as she drew back again.

"I wish I were home," she said huskily.

"In England, I mean. I wish I'd never agreed to come out here at all!"

"It's a bit late for wishing," Ryan said levelly. "Put it down to experience. At least you won't make the same mistake again." He waited a moment or two, then reached out suddenly and took the cigarette from her, nipping the end before tossing it into the wet shrubbery below. "You didn't really want that. Stop trying to be something you're not."

Gina said nothing, just stared at him blindly. The grey eyes took on a new expression as he looked down at her. Even before he got rid of his own cigarette the way he had got rid of hers, she knew he was going to take her in his arms.

He kissed her the way she had dreamed he would kiss her, not roughly, but not gently either, his mouth a moving, searching, mind-blanking entity that refused to be denied. Helplessly Gina found herself kissing him back, hands drifting up to tangle in the dark hair, body moulding itself against him, urged by the pressure of his hands sliding the length of her spine. Nothing concerned her outside of this moment. She wanted him to go on kissing her like this for ever.

The low rumbling sound deep in Pal's throat snapped them both out of it. The Alsatian was standing stiff-legged, gaze intent on the two of them. The amber eyes held a wild look in them.

Ryan eyed the dog for a brief, speculative moment, then let Gina go and called his name softly. A faint flick of the tawny tail acknowledged the command, but the animal made no other move to obey, standing his ground with a look of defiance in the set of his head.

"Jealousy," Ryan commented on an amused note. "But of which of us I'm not all that sure." He sharpened his tone. "Cut that out, feller!"

This time the dog gave way, sinking his head a little as he came slowly forward to put a tentative nose into his master's hand, plume of a tail dropped between his legs. Stooping, Ryan ran his other hand down between the flattened ears and over the long tan back, finishing up with a hard pat on the rump. "Watch yourself, boy," he said. "We don't want to ruin a fine relationship!"

The respite had given Gina time to take a hold of herself, although her breath and limbs were far from steady. When he turned back to her she was able to meet his eyes without flinching but could think of nothing to say. It was left to him to say it for both of them.

"I guess that put paid to that for the time being."

"Not just for the time being." She sounded rough but articulate. "Don't come near me again, Ryan. Not . . . like that."

"You don't mean that," he said, smiling a little. "You wanted it as much as I did. It certainly isn't the first time you've been kissed."

"Of course not."

"Then accept that it takes two to take it any further. Two people of the same mind."

Did it? thought Gina bleakly. His mind was more than enough for both of them should he make it up. She knew why he had kissed her. He was bored and she was the only game around. If she had rejected that advance he would probably have shrugged and left it at that. But she hadn't. She had responded, and with an immediacy which made her go hot to think about.

"I'm going to work," he said. "If you feel like making some coffee I'd be grateful for a mug."

"All right." She avoided his eyes. "Where will you be?"

"At my desk in the living room." Where else? his tone asked dryly.

"I'll bring it through when it's ready."

"Thanks."

He went off indoors, leaving her standing there a little forlornly. Pal was watching her with a peculiar expression. Uncertainty, she thought. She knew how he felt.

"Don't turn against me," she said very quietly. "I'm not trying to steal him from you, boy."

The dog dropped his head on to his

117

paws with an audible sigh of breath, obviously not about to respond to any appeal for understanding. Gina left well alone and went to make the coffee.

She could hear the typewriter from the kitchen. From the sound, he was a two-finger typist, but fast with it. When she took the coffee through to him he was studying a page of typescript with a frown between his eyes, scoring through a whole passage with a thick black pencil as she approached.

She said diffidently, "How's it going?" and received a faint wry smile as he glanced up.

"Predictably. As soon as I start reading through I want to scrap the whole thing and start over again."

"But you won't?"

"No. I don't have the time. I've a deadline in two weeks."

"Do you take it over to your publishers in person?" she asked, looking at the thick pile of manuscript.

"Definitely not. I see it in the post with

a sigh of relief and take off for parts unknown."

"To rest?"

He laughed. "No, I wouldn't say that exactly. If I don't already have an idea for my next book I start looking."

"Where do they come from?" Gina asked, fascinated. "The ideas, I mean."

"Oh—something you hear, something you see. There's no telling just when and where. The whole idea for *Thicker Than Water* came from a young Aussie I met down near Alice Springs. Twelve years old he was, and as big a misfit to that kind of life as I ever saw. He tried to bribe me to take him with me to Darwin when I left. If he'd been of age I might even have considered it. He was that desperate."

"And he became Sam who made his own way to the coast at sixteen and founded a commercial empire," Gina said reminiscently. "I loved that book—all but the ending. Why did you have to kill him off?"

"Because that was the way it went," came the sardonic comment. "Life isn't always as neat as you'd obviously like it to be."

"I know, but you're a writer. You can make your characters do anything you want them to."

"Don't you believe it. I didn't know Sam was going to die that way when I started the book. I knew..." He stopped, face closing up as if he regretted having said as much as he had. "It isn't important. It's a long time ago."

And that particular novel had topped the best-selling lists for nearly nine months, in addition to being filmed, Gina recalled wryly. "Sorry," she said. "I didn't mean it to sound like criticism."

He glanced up at her then, face changing expression yet again, this time to a self-directed irony. "That's okay. I'm getting over-sensitive."

"Only because I was being particularly obtuse."

He was silent for a moment, studying her with an odd look in his eyes. "I'll be through here for the day after lunch," he said. "If the weather keeps on improving

I'll take you round the island. It isn't big, but it does have rather a lot going for it."

She was taken aback by the offer but not enough to turn it down. She wanted to be with him, she acknowledged. After today she might never again have the chance.

She took a walk down to the nearer beach after she had left him, wanting time away from the house to think. A watery sunlight broke from the cloud as she made her way along the overgrown path, strengthening by the minute as the patch of blue sky widened. The wind was still stiff enough to put white caps on the waves beyond the reef, but this side of it the water was beginning to look quite calm again, breaking almost clear of the boat lying where she had beached it—was it really only yesterday?

The long deep gouges decorating the fibreglass bottom made her wince. One of them went almost all the way through. It would need patching up before anyone could sail it at all, and no doubt that would be a costly enough job, to say nothing of making the vessel wholly shipshape again. She was thankful she was going to have someone like Ryan behind her. At least he knew how to handle matters.

Sitting down in a sheltered spot beside a crooked cabbage palm, she clasped her arms about bent legs and rested her forehead on her bare knees, trying to sort out the confusion inside her. Yet was she really so confused when she came down to it? Why not admit the truth—that she was on the verge of falling in love with a man she had known bare hours in totality. It had started the other night if she were honest about it. Odd, but she had never believed in love at first sight before. Except that it hadn't been first sight, had it? She had known that face and followed his career for several months before this. And why? Because something about him had attracted her even on paper. Not that she had ever imagined that one day she might meet him, much less find herself stranded on a tiny island with him. It was a romantic situation, she supposed. Perhaps some time he might even use it in a book.

She hoped not, though, because it meant something to her even if it didn't mean a great deal to him.

The sky was almost fully cleared by the time she went back to the house, the sun beating down on her bare head. Ryan was sitting out on the verandah, Pal at his feet. He watched her coming without visible change of expression.

"Made a mess of her, didn't you?" he commented as she approached. "Nothing that can't be repaired, of course, but fibreglass takes special equipment."

"You don't have to rub it in," she came back wryly. "I still don't see that I had much choice—unless you think I should have stayed and accepted what I'd asked for."

He shrugged. "You might have found your would-be rapist had come to his senses after a night's sleep. Either that or he'd found satisfaction somewhere else. There's usually no shortage of willing partners at one of those affairs."

Gina looked at him sharply. "Have you been to one of them yourself?"

"Not my style. They're pretty notorious around these parts, though."

"Then why don't the authorities do something about it? Surely . . ."

"It's a privately owned island," he said. "Nobody complains, so nobody investigates."

"Who owns it?"

"Someone you'd have done well to steer clear of. Slade Harley runs the biggest callgirl racket in the islands."

"And the authorities still do nothing?"

"There's no proof. To get a conviction they'd need somebody to testify. Anybody on his payroll who tried it would disappear pretty quickly."

Gina shivered suddenly. "Do those kind of things really happen?"

"All over the world, not just here. Don't let it concern you, you're out of it."

"It has to concern me. I left Marie on that island."

"I'd say she can take care of Number One quite adequately. Salad and cold ham okay for lunch?"

"Yes, lovely." She had to smile a little. "You're very well organised, aren't you?"

"I don't starve for my art," he returned easily. "On the other hand, I find these few months a healthy interlude from the rest of the year's excesses. Wine, women and song—they all go by the board."

"Not song, surely," she said, tongue in cheek. "You've a record-player and quite a stack of records."

"Not women either this time round. You're the first one I ever had here."

His tone was devoid of any ulterior meaning. Gina gave him the benefit of the doubt. "Uninvited, you mean?"

"I mean the very first. The place is sacrosanct to all but Neil whenever I'm here."

"And now I've spoiled the record."

"There's a first time for everything." He stood up, tall, lean and enigmatic. "Let's go and eat."

It was gone two before they were ready to take the promised walk. Ryan found an old straw hat and insisted Gina wear it, smiling when she protested.

"Vanity? You don't have to worry. There's something appealing about that get-up of yours. Maybe because they're my things and you're wearing them. You could always put your bikini back on, though."

"It doesn't matter," she said hurriedly. "I just don't think I need a hat."

"Then you'll just have to take my word for it."

As he had said, the island was small but beautiful. His own small cabin cruiser was beached in the shelter of an almost landlocked lagoon, the latter like a brochure illustration with its whiter-than-white sand and green vegetation.

"They should have built the house here," said Gina, viewing the lovely spot. "I wonder why they didn't."

"I've often wondered the same thing myself," Ryan acknowledged. "If I lived here on a regular basis I'd consider rebuilding, but for three months of a year it isn't worth it—especially as I spend most of my time at the typewriter."

"How long is it," she asked, "since you first came here to write?"

"Roughly four years. I've been writing for ten."

"What did you do before that?"

"Various things. I was a wanderer." His smile came and went. "What former novelists would have called a wastrel. My father left me too adequately provided for. I didn't have to work for a living." His glance came back to her. "What about you? Your parents still alive?"

She shook her head. "Dad died when I was quite young, Mom a couple of years ago."

"So you're on your own now?"

"Completely." She infused cheerfulness into her voice. "The last of the Tierson line!"

"And that will go when you marry."

"If I ever do."

His lips twisted. "I shouldn't think there's much doubt. It seems to be the overall female ambition."

"We're not all the same," she retorted, stung to swift anger. "Don't generalise!"

"I'll try to remember." It was said with satire. "We'll go this way. There's another beach across the other side of the island with a fine variety of shells, if you're interested in anything like that."

The anger died as swiftly as it had arisen. She said ruefuly, "I seem to spend all my time apologising to you."

He laughed, humour apparently restored. "Better that way than the other way round." His hand came on to her shoulder, turning her ahead of him along the path, his whistle bringing Pal trotting back from his explorations to bound ahead of them both. Ryan let the hand lie there lightly as he drew abreast of her, his bent arm resting against her back in a gesture she found heartwarmingly intimate. She didn't want him to let her go, but he did after a moment or two.

It took them little more than twenty minutes to make the other beach via the centre of the island. From the top of the low prominence, Gina looked out over a vista of white-capped ocean and wondered at her luck in fetching up on this tiny speck of land.

"Why do you choose this part of the year to work?" she asked as they descended the far side. "It must be dangerous at times."

"I don't *choose* any part of the year," he said. "Depends when I have enough material together to feel like making a serious start. This time it just happened to run to this particular period. The only real danger would be if I found myself in the path of a hurricane. Not that one of those is any picnic wherever you happen to be. Anyway, I do have a radio for essential broadcasts, and there's usually enough warning given."

"But don't you ever feel lonely?"

"Not when I'm actually writing— maybe occasionally when I'm not. But like I said, I pop across to Nassau once a week and live it up with Neil."

"He's quite a bit older than you, I imagine."

"Nine years. I met him in the States five years ago. He was the one who told me about this place. Before that I used to write wherever I happened to be at the time the urge came over me—not always very easily."

"Because of the interruptions?"

"Very much so. People can't get it through their heads that writing's a job like any other. They think because you're there you're available for a chat or a drink or anything else whenever they happen to feel in the mood. I know one married author who got himself an office in town and goes there eight till five, five days a week, because it's the only way he can get any work done. I know just how he feels."

Gina said lightly, "Is that why you're staying a bachelor yourself?"

"Not especially. I just never found the woman I'd want to spend the rest of my life with, and I can't see the point in bothering on the basis that divorce is easy if it doesn't work out." His smile was dry. "Anyway, she'd have to be pretty unusual to contemplate spending three months of every year here."

"She could always stay in Nassau, I suppose," she said on the same light note.

"No way. It's the nights here I find the loneliest."

"In other words, she would have to be a mouse by day and a wife only at night. You want everything your own way."

"That's right. And as I'm unlikely to get what I want on that score, I don't intend trying."

"Defeatism," she said.

"No, practicality. Here we are."

This beach lacked the soft beauty of the lagoon but made up for it with a variety of sea refuse Gina found fascinating.

"There's a strong current around the headland which seems to carry everything up here," Ryan explained. "If you'd got caught in that you'd have finished up on this side of the island too. It's doubtful if I'd have seen you."

"I was lucky," she said. "Right the way through I was lucky. I don't know a thing about boats—or the sea."

"Or men?" He was standing close behind her; so close she could feel his breath on her hair. When his hands slid about her waist she stiffened but didn't move away, letting him draw her back against him and feeling the quivering start deep. Only when he moved his hands slowly up her body to cover the firm curve of her breasts through the thin material of her shirt did she make any kind of protest, and even then her voice sounded anything but decisive.

"Don't, Ryan . . . please!"

He said softly, "You're saying that for the sake of it, Gina. You want me to hold you like this." The brushing caress of his thumbs across her nipples made her ache. "Even if you won't say it, these say it for you. They've taunted me all day under that shirt of mine. Watching you move around, knowing that's all you have on— it's enough to drive any man crazy!"

"No!" It was more plea than denial, her whole body longing for the long brown fingers to continue their exploration even as her mind rejected his advances. She put up trembling hands and seized his, feeling the sinews in his wrists contract as she attempted to pull them away from her.

He laughed and put his lips to the side of her neck where he had pushed away the hair, lightly scoring a passage downwards with the tip of his tongue, making her skin tingle and burn as if scorched by fire. "You really want me to stop?"

"Yes." It was a whisper.

"All right." He let her go, stepping away from her. "That better?"

"Yes," she said again. She wanted to turn round and face him but was not sufficiently in control of herself to risk it. His easy compliance hurt more than anything. He was simply playing with her the way a cat plays with a mouse, watching her writhe with the same cruel calculation. "Can't you leave anyone alone?" she asked fiercely. "Do you have to prove what a virile man you are with every woman you meet?"

"No," he said. "Only those who attract me. *I'm* not going to rape you, Gina. I've never found it necessary to use force on a woman, and I'm not about to start now."

She could believe it. If he really set his mind to it he could no doubt overcome any resistance. Only she wasn't going to give him the chance. For her own sake, she had to keep him away from her.

"I'm going back," he said on a casual note which made her want to swing round and hit him. "Coming?"

She had to turn then, only to find him already walking away. That was as much as the last few minutes had meant to him. In that moment was born in her the urge to make him suffer the same emotional strain she had just suffered—to make him want her, *really* want her, and then turn round and walk away as he was doing now. It wouldn't be easy, but she'd do it if it killed her!

# 5

S HE caught him up at the bottom of the slope, falling into place at his side with an air of unconcern which drew a quizzical glance from him.

"Decided to forgive me my trespasses?" he said satirically.

"You took me by surprise," she said, keeping her head bent to watch the path ahead for obstacles. "I'm not used to men like you."

"You're not used to men, period. What has it been up to now—holding hands in the cinema; a few stolen kisses in a parked car?"

"Something like that, I suppose. It's hardly my fault that the people I meet don't happen to live the kind of life-style you do—or theirs either, for that matter."

"So now your curiosity's aroused. What would it be like to be made love to by a man of experience!"

"Don't mock me," she said, and drew a faint smile.

"If anything I was mocking myself. I took advantage of an unwary moment back there. The temptation, as you might say, proved too strong."

"It almost did for me too," she confessed. "Just because I never did it before it doesn't mean I never wanted to."

"Moral obligations?" he suggested.

"I suppose so. I was convent-educated. It makes a difference."

"But you don't plan on holding out for marriage before you take the plunge."

"I don't know." The pause was timed. "I did."

He stopped walking with an abruptness that surprised her, taking her by the shoulders and turning her towards him with deliberation. The grey eyes scanned her face narrowly. "Do you know what you're saying?"

"Yes." Her heart was thudding against her ribs, but the need to get to him was stronger than any doubts his expression could conjure. "Yes, I know.

I—I can't help it, Ryan."

"Let me get this quite straight. You want me to make love to you?"

She forced herself to say it. "Yes."

"Why?"

"Because nobody ever roused me to the extent you can. Because I think with you it could be something really great, and that's how I want the first time to be."

"That's not the impression you gave me down on the beach."

"I told you, it was too quick. You scared me a little."

"But I don't scare you now?"

"No."

"Then prove it."

She stared at him, unable to control her reaction for a fleeting moment. "Here?"

"Why not? We're not likely to be interrupted."

"Yes, we are." She saw Pal coming back down the path with relief. "You're forgetting your jealous friend over there."

"So I am. Pity about that." He reached out and drew a knuckle gently down her cheek, mouth curving. "I'll be glad to oblige at a more opportune moment. Tonight, for instance. Do we have a date?"

Her throat felt dry. "Yes," she got out.

"I'll count on it." He gestured to the approaching dog. "Okay, we're on our way!"

Doubt threatened to swamp her as he moved on ahead. Was she taking on a little more than she could handle? she wondered. But he had made that statement down on the beach, and she believed it. He wouldn't use force. He wouldn't demean himself.

Gina would have given anything for a cup of hot tea when they finally reached the house again, but there didn't appear to be any and she didn't care to ask. She settled for iced lime juice instead, sitting out on the verandah with Ryan and Pal to watch the sky begin to turn that opaque shade of blue which heralded the approach of nightfall at these latitudes. Already the birds were settling in the trees, the cicadas increasing their decibel rate as if in competition with the twittering and chirping and fluttering of wings. Since first coming to the islands, Gina had loved this time of day the best, sitting out on the balcony back at the hotel until the last light went from the sky and the balmy evening breeze wafted in the fragrant darkness.

It was like that here too, only more so, because there were no extraneous noises to spoil the effect. She felt she could sit forever just listening and looking, feeling the delicious coolness settle over her body after the heat of the afternoon.

"I'm going for a swim," Ryan said suddenly. "Coming?" She looked at him, startled out of her reverie to the realisation that she was not alone. "Won't it be too rough still?"

"Not in the lagoon. I swim there most nights. It's safe enough."

She hesitated a moment longer, then slowly shook her head. "I think I'll stay here. I don't feel like making the effort to change."

He lifted an eyebrow and seemed about to say something else, but apparently changed his mind, clicking his tongue to

Pal instead. "Okay, I'll see you in a little while. I'll be fetching a lobster out of the keeper cage, so don't start preparing anything for dinner. You do like lobster, I hope?"

She nodded. "Love it!"

"Good—it doesn't agree with everybody. You might put a bottle of wine to chill. You'll find a rack behind the store room door." He gave her a final glance and lifted a hand in faintly smiling farewell. "Don't go away."

There was nowhere for her to go; she was beginning to wish there was. The urge which had driven her all afternoon was starting to fade, replaced by mingled trepidation and regret. What she had planned had seemed quite feasible in the light of day, but the darkness brought a new element.

So back out now while there was still time, common sense urged her. She could tell Ryan she had changed her mind. She wasn't even all that certain just how far she would have to go to get him to the point at which rejection would really reckon with him. And would he be prepared to let her get away with it if she did try rejecting him? What he said and what he might do could be two different things. Dared she take that risk for the sake of hurt pride?

Still undecided, she went to find the wine and put it in the chilling rack on the refrigerator door. The label meant nothing to her, though no doubt it was a good one. Wasted on her, she reflected wryly, because she had no particular palate for wines, except for knowing that she preferred white to red and dry rather than sweet. Apart from that, they all tasted much the same.

The moon wasn't risen yet, but out here that made little difference as the stars were bright enough to see one's way by. On impulse, she followed in Ryan's footsteps along the path to the lagoon, coming on the gleaming crescent of beach with a sense of wonder at its sheer beauty.

Ryan was about halfway between shore and reef, his head a dark blob against the silver-streaked water. Beside him, and keeping pace, swam Pal, the two of them obviously well accustomed to bathing together. Even as she watched, they made the turn to start coming in again, the dog's head lifted clear of the water, ears laid back. There was a paler flash as Ryan disappeared below the water, and a pause that seemed alarmingly long before his head broke surface again. Gina saw he was carrying some object in one hand, holding it away from his body as he swam sidestroke for the shore.

The two of them reached the shallows in unison and found their feet, the dog splashing clear of the waves to stand and shake before spinning about with a deep-throated challenge. Ryan laughed, and scooped up a pebble to throw for the dog, standing with feet planted slightly apart for balance as the water swirled about them watching the animal chase along the sand, the lobster still held at arm's length. That he was accustomed to bathing and sunbathing in the nude was evidenced by the lack of any demarcation line about his hips. Outlined against the sky he looked magnificent; modern man returned to Nature.

Pal came back to drop the retrieved pebble at his feet and stand back in panting anticipation, but Ryan shook his head, coming further up the beach to where he had left his clothes. Gina took a hasty step back into the deeper shadows as he reached for his shorts, leaning against a ridged trunk and trying to come to terms with the feelings running riot inside her. This island could be a paradise for lovers; a private haven where nothing else mattered but being together. How marvellous to run into the sea like that, to feel the silky warmth against one's skin with nothing to trap or hamper; to shed all inhibitions in glorious, heavenly freedom. If only—

She held her breath, hearing his approach, only now remembering Pal and the likelihood of discovery. He was past before the dog scented her, and even then might have carried on had a single whine of recognition not escaped the furry throat. Dismay filled her as she saw him turn and look back along the path, probing the shadows to see what had attracted the Alsatian's attention. Then he was moving towards her and it was too late to do anything but stand and face it out.

"I'm sorry," she said low-toned. "I didn't realise you . . ."

"Swam in the buff?" he finished for her as her voice trailed away. He sounded unperturbed. "Why didn't you come and join me?"

"Just like that?"

He laughed. "Why not just like that? The water felt great tonight. You'd have enjoyed it."

"And you wouldn't have cared." The words were torn from her.

It was a moment before he answered. He looked very big and powerful in the darkness under the trees, his expression impossible to read. "Naturally I'd have cared," he said at length. "But it wouldn't have happened right there and then because I wouldn't have wanted it to. I'm going to take you to bed, Gina—tonight after supper. We're going to make love in

144

comfort, and with time on our hands to enjoy it the way it should be enjoyed. That's what you wanted, isn't it?"

Now was the time to tell him, but she couldn't find the words. She could hear the sound of her heart thudding into her ears, feel the racing of her pulses. He seemed to take her silence for agreement, indicating the path ahead of him with a nod of his head.

"Careful of this feller. He didn't like being jerked out of a stupor."

Gina skirted the lobster with caution and walked on in front, lower lip caught between her teeth. Somehow she was going to have to find the right moment to admit she had been making believe. She only hoped she would recognise it when it came. One thing was certain: it had to be before they finished supper.

"Gina," Ryan said softly at her back, "when we reach the house go and put on your bikini and wrap, will you? Those things of mine don't do you justice."

She couldn't find a word to say to that

either. Not right now. She needed time to think.

They sat down at eight to a meal superbly prepared and presented, the accompanying salad tossed in a dressing which was Ryan's own concoction and tasted delicious.

"An occasional hobby of mine," he said when Gina complimented him on the meal. He reached over and refilled her wine-glass, face shadowed by the flickering light of the candles. His smile was all she could see with any clarity, warm and intimate.

"Like it?" he asked.

She nodded, aware that it wasn't the wine itself so much as the effect it was having on her. She needed dutch courage to face what she had to face, and she needed it soon. If he once took her in his arms again it might very well be too late.

"You're very quiet," he said. "What are you thinking?"

"Nothing." She tried to smile, unable to dissemble very far. "I mean, nothing specific."

"You're wondering what it's going to be like between us, is that it?" He moved aside the bowl of fresh fruit which had served them for dessert and reached for her hand, drawing it towards him and holding it in a light clasp. "All right, I'll tell you. In a little while from now, when the moment is right, I'm going to come round there and lift you from that chair and take you to bed. There'll be no hurry because we've got all the time in the world —a whole night ahead of us. At first I'll just hold you, kiss you a little; caress you. When I undress you it will be gradually, one garment at a time, until I finally hold the whole lovely length of you in my arms. And you'll do the same for me, my darling. Not because you have to but because you'll want to; because you'll need to know me the way I'll know you by then—every curve, every line, every last part of you."

The low intimacy of his voice was reaching depths she had not known existed in her, the exquisitely gentle stroking movement of a finger tip against the sensitive inner skin of her palm sending small tremors through her. She listened like someone in a trance, reacting as much to the pitch and timbre as to the words themselves. Did all men of his kind talk this way to a woman, she wondered blindly, or was the gift his and his alone? Was he aware just how far and fast such arousal went? Yes, of course he was. He knew everything there was to know about making a woman want him. And want him she did, with everything in her: achingly, yearningly, transcending all doubt. Tomorrow had no bearing, only tonight . . . tonight . . .

She saw him rise through a haze, felt him draw her to her feet and gently towards him. Then she was in his arms with his lips on hers, his hand sliding down and under her knees to lift her up across his chest.

She clung to him as he carried her to the door, turning her face into his shoulder to inhale the male scent of him. One of her sandals slipped off, and then the other, falling to the floor without impeding his movement. Her own bedroom door was half open, the room beyond in darkness. He closed it behind him with a lifted foot before taking her over to lay her down on the bed.

Gina closed her eyes as his weight came down beside her. He gathered her close, but not too close, putting his lips to the point of her jawline close to her ear and feathering them slowly downwards until he finally found her mouth. No pressure at first; he seemed almost to play with her lips, teasing them gently apart, making her relax and respond at one and the same time. Even had she wanted to she would have found him impossible to resist, his dominance too complete.

His hands were tender on her skin, tracing the curve of her body from breast to thigh in a way which brought every nerve ending alive. Possessive too, making her feel she belonged to him, and only him. When he slid off the flimsy jacket and lowered his head to kiss the top of her breasts she knew a last, fleeting renewal of doubt, but it was too late now; she could find neither the words nor the will to stop him.

She felt his hand slide behind her back and unclip the single fastening, easing the covering material away from her until she lay defenceless under his gaze. The touch of his tongue brought a faint gasp to her lips, her body arching towards him, her own hands sliding around his back and over taut muscles to run the length of his spine with an instinctive, feather-light touch which made him catch his breath.

"I want you," she whispered. "Oh, Ryan, I want you!" His reply was anything but soft. "I know. Hell, isn't it?"

She lay frozen as he pushed himself up and away from her, unable to grasp what had happened to him—unable to think straight at all. He had wanted her too, that had been apparent. So why this sudden change?

She said it out loud. "Why?"

"You despise people like me, remember?" He gave her a raking glance, lips curling as she brought her arms swiftly across to cover herself. "Too late for that this time. Be grateful I left you the rest."

"You planned it all," she whispered, still unbelieving. "Ever since last night you've been planning this!"

"That's right, I planned it." His tone was hard. "Putting you in your place, I think you called it. How do you like it?" He put out a hand and pressed her down again as she attempted to sit up, holding her still with a light but firm pressure. "No running away till you've heard what *I* have to say."

"Haven't you said enough?" Her throat hurt so much she could hardly force the words out. There was a burning sensation behind her eyes, but she had never felt further from tears. "You made your point. I was an easy target, wasn't I!"

"You didn't put up much of a fight, true. Not that I intended to let you. Retaliation should be immediate if possible, but I gave you the benefit of twenty-four hours."

"That makes it worse, not better!"

"For you perhaps. Personally, I've

enjoyed every minute. It's a bit like fishing for tuna. You hook a fine one and start reeling it in, then it makes a run and you play it along, all the time drawing it closer and closer until it's finally lying alongside ready for the net."

"Stop it!" Gina fought against the hand holding her, but it refused to let her go. Limbs trembling, she finally desisted, lying there looking at him with eyes dark with loathing. "You swine! You calculating swine!"

"Hell hath no fury," he misquoted, unmoved. "If it's any consolation I'm not getting away unscathed myself. There was a moment back there when I almost went over the top. You've a lovely body, honey. I'd have liked to know all of it as well as I know these beautiful breasts of yours. Unfortunately, the only way to make you suffer frustration was to suffer it myself. The price one must pay."

"You didn't have to go this far," she said thickly. "If I got to you so badly last night you could have told me then what you thought of me."

"You don't listen to mere words," he said. "Not unless they're underlined with a little action. Even then, if I'd grabbed you like this last night you'd have been so busy spitting fire you wouldn't have got the message. This way it comes through loud and clear. In future watch what you're saying and who you're saying it to. Not all of us subscribe to the privileged sex theme." He paused then, studying her face with a twist of his lips. "Nothing left to say?"

"Just go away and leave me alone." Her voice shook. "You got what you wanted. Now get out!"

"I said watch it." He got to his feet, running a last lingering glance over the length of her with a look of mock regret. "I'd better go while I still have that much will power left. It could have been really something!"

At the door he paused, looking back at her. "We'll be leaving right after breakfast, all being well: Be ready."

Whole minutes passed before Gina could bring herself to make any move after

153

he had gone. She felt sick, the taut misery in her chest threatening to overflow. Whether she had asked for what had happened or not was immaterial. The point was that it had happened at all. Twenty-four hours, Ryan had said. That was all it had taken to bring her down to this. How could she face herself again?

They landed at eleven on the same beach Gina had left three days previously. A man about to descend to the ski-deck of the jetty paused to give her a startled glance as she stepped ashore from Ryan's cabin cruiser.

"Aren't you the girl who's been missing?" he queried curiously. "There's a search plane out looking for your boat right now." His eyes flickered to Ryan and back again. "Story was you were on your own when the storm hit."

"She was," Ryan said shortly. He took Gina's arm in a light grasp, resisting her immediate attempt to shake it off with a grim tilt of his lips. "Try acting like an

154

adult for once. We have to get the search called off."

For Gina the following fifteen minutes were confused ones. Despite everything, she was glad of Ryan's calm support throughout the ordeal of questions and phone calls in the hotel manager's office. She had a distinct impression of scepticism behind the latter's acceptance of her story, especially from the way his glance kept drifting from her to Ryan during the telling of it.

Marie's arrival from wherever she had been located was another ordeal.

"We got back yesterday," she said. "They had a radio transmitter at the house, so we knew you hadn't made it back before the storm struck. We were all pretty sure you'd capsized the boat." She gave Ryan a frankly speculative glance. "Lucky she happened to land up in your place, wasn't it?"

"Yes," he agreed, "it was." The grey eyes held a cynical expression. "Can you put me in touch with these people who own the launch? She'll need working on before she can be put in the water again."

"I can give you a number to ring." Her gaze shifted a little as if she found him disconcerting. To Gina she added with a certain faint relish. "There's going to be trouble over that boat, I'm afraid. You should never have taken it."

"There won't be any trouble," Ryan said with an assurance which comforted Gina in spite of her doubts. He glanced at her briefly. "Why don't you go and change? I'll deal with it."

"It isn't your responsibility," she came back stiffly, aware of Marie's observation. "I should . . ."

"I said I'd deal with it." He turned back to the manager. "Mind if I do it from here?"

"Certainly, Mr. Barras." It was apparent from the man's manner that if any blame was to be attached he preferred to be well clear. "I'll see to it that you're not disturbed."

Outside he said to Gina, "I'm afraid the police might want to question you, Miss

Tierson. There was a full-scale search mounted yesterday when the weather cleared. That's a costly exercise, you know."

"I couldn't help it," she said. "There was no way I could let anyone know I was all right."

"I realise that, and I'm sure they will too. It's just a formality, as I said." Having made his point he unbent a little. "Fortunately we hadn't taken the step of informing next of kin."

Gina didn't bother informing him of her lack of family; it was irrelevant now. Wearily she accompanied Marie across the entrance lounge to the lifts, trying to ignore the glances she was receiving from all sides and hoping no one would take it into their heads to ask for details. She couldn't, she just *couldn't* go through the story again.

They reached the bedroom without that happening. Only then, with the door closed, did Marie give way to the questions obviously burning a hole in her mind.

"Talk about falling on your feet!" she

exclaimed. "Imagine meeting up with him again—and marooned on an island too! It's almost unbelievable!"

Gina sat down on the end of her bed. "It's true," she said unemotionally. "Marie, what happened after I left?"

"We woke up and found the boat gone, that's what happened." The other girl's regard held a curious mixture of emotions. "Why did you have to go and do a fool thing like that? Rafe was going to bring us back at night, like he said, but we couldn't find you anywhere."

"Sven tried to rape me." Even to her own ears the words sounded faintly ridiculous spoken here in this room in broad daylight. From Marie's expression it was apparent that she thought so too, "Oh, come on!" she said deridingly. "He might have fancied his chances, but that's laying it on a bit thick."

"You weren't there." Gina shuddered at the memory. "He was drunk. I got away from him and hid out above the beach all night. I didn't plan on taking the boat— it was a spur-of-the-moment idea."

"Dear is what it's going to cost you too."

"From those two?" Gina sounded more confident than she felt. "I doubt if they'll be bringing any charges. After all, it was Sven I was running from."

"It's your word against his, and you went out there willingly enough." Marie left no room for a reply. "Anyway, the boat doesn't actually belong to either of them. It's on a kind of semi-permanent loan from the man they both work for. He's the one your friend downstairs is going to have to deal with, and he won't find that such easy going."

"You know this man?"

There was a subtle change of expression in Marie's eyes. "Yes," she said, "I know him. You'd have met him too if you hadn't been in such a hurry to leave the party. He brought us all back on his own boat yesterday."

"Rich?" Gina hazarded, and received a faint smile. "Very."

"Then you found what you were looking for."

"Not quite. He's not the marrying type."

"That's a shame."

"Isn't it." Her shrug was dismissive. "I daresay I'll make out."

"I'm sure you will." Gina lost interest in the exchange, brows drawing together. "Marie, do you really think he's going to make a lot of trouble? I know I took the boat without permission, but I didn't know there was going to be a storm."

"I'm not exactly sure what he'll do," Marie acknowledged. "All I do know is that the insurance covers theft but not voluntary loan to incompetents. Work it out for yourself. Rich or not, he's going to want some form of compensation if the boat's in as big a mess as you say it is."

"It may not be as bad as it looks," said Gina, trying to convince herself. "And Ryan said he could fix things."

"You hardly know the man. What makes you so sure he can fix anything?" The pause was timed. "Unless you two got a whole lot closer than you're letting on.

Amazing what a man will let himself in for if he's asked at the right moment."

A knock on the outer door saved Gina from trying to find a suitably scathing reply. She knew she had flushed, and that Marie had noted it. She called "Come in" in a voice that sounded pinched.

It was Ryan. He came into the room and closed the door, looking at Gina with a closed expression.

"I thought you were going to get some clothes on."

"I was." She came to her feet, her baser emotions almost cancelling out the immediate uncertainty. "Did you . . . speak to anyone?"

"Yes," he said. "He wants to see you."

"He's going to make trouble over what happened?"

"No, that's all fixed. He just wants to see you."

"Why?"

"Ask him. I said I'd take you over there for lunch."

"You know him?"

"I know of him. I never met him before

161

today." There was a hard note to his voice. "If you'd rather go like that . . ."

"I'd rather not go at all," she stated with a hardness of her own. "Is it absolutely necessary?"

"Unless you want to finish up discussing the distinction between stealing and borrowing with the authorities instead."

"I just can't see any point," she said stubbornly. "Either he's going to drop it or he isn't. What difference is my going to see him going to make?"

"Call it a whim on his part."

Her head lifted. "Well, I'm not going."

"You are." He said it quietly but with a determination Gina had to recognise. "He made it a condition. Find some clothes and get them on."

Gina watched him sit down in the chair by the door with a sense of impotency. "I'm not changing with you in the room," she said, "There's the bathroom," he pointed out. "You've got about fifteen minutes. It's a fair distance round the Point."

Marie shrugged as Gina glanced swiftly

her way. "Don't look at me. Better do as the man says."

There didn't seem much choice. In silence, Gina gathered together a few items of clothing she was going to need and took them into the bathroom. Only when she heard Marie speak did she realise she hadn't quite closed the door. She went to do it, pausing on hearing Ryan's answer.

"You weren't invited."

Marie said, "You mean my name wasn't mentioned at all."

"It was mentioned," he said. "But not in that connection." The pause was brief, his tone when he spoke again con-temptuous. "You know what kind of set-up you're getting into?"

"It isn't like that. Not for me."

"What makes you different?"

"Why don't you ask Slade that your-self?"

"He has a personal interest?"

"I don't see why that should make you smile." Her tone changed a little, became softer. "You don't think I have what it takes to attract a man like Slade Harley?"

"On the contrary, I'm sure you have exactly what it takes. You're playing out of your league, that's all."

"What is my league? Your friend Neil?" She laughed. "Give him my regards when you see him again." There was a pause, and her tone changed again. "Where do you fit in, anyway?"

"I don't. It isn't my league either."

"You're taking Gina out to the house."

"On a temporary basis only, and because I couldn't get out of it."

"But why? Why does Slade want to see her?"

"Apparently he's curious. Girls who subscribe to the 'Fate worse than death' theme are in short supply out here."

"They're in short supply everywhere. Trust me to pick out one of the few!"

Ryan said steadily, "Considering your reasons for coming out here, I'm surprised you found any need of a companion at all. Or did you think a lone female might look a mite too predatory?"

"It could have been something like that." Marie was obviously not about

164

to let herself be put down. "You two certainly had some cosy little chats on that island of yours. I noticed she didn't do any subscribing with *your* boat!"

"Once bitten, twice shy. She was lucky to live through the first escape."

"Oh, you admit there was something for her to escape from then?"

"If you like to put that construction on it." He sounded unmoved.

Gina closed the door with a snick she hoped they both heard. She had listened to enough—more than enough! There had been cynicism in his voice when he had said that about a fate worse than death. He knew, if Marie didn't, how far from that league she belonged. Emotionally she felt dead, at least where Ryan was concerned. She couldn't even hate him.

Marie had gone from the bedroom when she finally went out. Ryan tossed down the magazine he had heen flicking through and came to his feet, giving her simple blue cotton dress an approving nod.

"Very appropriate. That should convince him if nothing else does."

"Convince who?" she said, acting dumb.

"Slade Harley, the man you're going to see."

"Oh, your gangster friend."

"Don't play the fool," he said tautly. "This isn't my choice, it's his. As the injured party he's entitled to make conditions."

"What about my side of it?" she demanded. "I could lay charges against his employees."

"What charges? You went with them of your own free will."

"I didn't know it was going to be an orgy!"

"It was a private party on a private island. There's only your word for it that anything orgiastic was going on."

Meeting the cynical grey eyes, Gina felt her throat close up. "All right," she said wearily. "So I'll do the right thing."

"Good." He nodded towards the door. "Let's go."

"Why involve yourself in all this?" she

166

asked without moving. "You don't owe me anything."

The sudden glitter was dangerous. "Call it good deed week. If you'll take some advice, you'll pack your things when you get back here and take the next plane for home."

"I can't," she said. "The fare structure we came out under doesn't allow for any chopping and changing."

"Then pay the excess."

"I can't afford it."

The look he gave her held a curious kind of resignation. "Just how much do you have left?"

"That's none of your business."

"I'm making it my business."

"Then you can whistle! I got myself here, I'll get myself back!"

Ryan made no move towards her, just stood there looking at her for a moment with the same odd expression. "I really made you hate me last night, didn't I?" he said.

"No," she forced herself to meet his eyes without flinching. "You taught me to trust my initial instincts about people in future. You're a better writer than you are a human being."

"Amen," he said dryly. His shoulders lifted. "Water under the bridge. Let's get moving."

Gina had expected to drive to wherever they were going, but instead they took the boat westwards along the coast past Balmoral Island to Delaport Point. Their destination was a sea-front property built in the Spanish style, white walls shimmering in the heat through the fringe of swaying casuarinas. A man appeared from the shady side of a large boathouse as they reached the shore end of the landing stage. He was a Nassauvian in the mid to late twenties, face impassive as he waited for them to reach him. Despite the heat he was wearing a double-breasted suit in dark blue along with a bright pink shirt and tie.

"You come this way," he said shortly, and turned to head towards the house without further preamble.

Walking beside Ryan in the wake of

their guide, Gina stole a glance at the lean profile, but there was nothing to be gleaned from his expression. If he was prepared to take things as they came then so must she. A long terrace ran along the seaward side of the house, shaded by awnings which pulled down in sections. Here a table had been set for lunch with three places. Their host moved to greet them from the top of the stone steps leading up from the gardens, dark-skinned features creased in a disarming smile. He was a big, handsome man about forty-five years of age, his hair black and curly. The amber-tinted eyes were hypnotic.

"Glad you could make it," he said, as if there had been any other choice. His voice was cultured, deep and pleasant on the ear. His gaze resting on Gina held a glint of something other than mere appraisement. "So this is the one."

"I'm sorry about damaging your boat," she said evenly, and felt a sudden surge of defiance sweep through her. "But not about taking it," she added. "In a way you're responsible. It was one of your employees I was trying to get away from."

"So I understand." He appeared more amused than resentful. "He has already been reprimanded for his lack of—discernment, shall we call it?—but if you would prefer a more personal apology?"

"No, it's all right." Gina couldn't bear the thought of seeing Sven again under any circumstances. She had made her stance and that was enough. "I suppose I should never have gone with him in the first place," she conceded.

"No," he agreed on a dry note. He turned his attention to Ryan eyes taking on a different expression. "And the launch is now beached on this island north-east of here? You think the damage can be repaired on the spot?"

"Patched up," said Ryan. "She shipped very little water considering. Interior damage should be minimal."

The gesture was dismissive. "We shall see. A drink before we eat?"

Lunch, Gina had to admit, was not the ordeal she had anticipated. Served by a silently efficient, white-coated Negro, the food was superb, the accompanying wines recognisable even to her untutored palate as of the best. And their host was charming, channeling conversation along lines which left no one sitting by with nothing to contribute and generally making every effort to entertain. She could see why Marie found him such a draw. Even without the added financial attraction, he was a man many women would find devastating.

He had read several of Ryan's books, and made intelligent comment with an interest to which few could have failed to respond, watching the other man's face with those penetrating amber eyes all the time he was speaking.

"You haven't written a book set in this area of the world yet," he remarked lightly at one point. "I wonder why? The material is all around you."

Ryan shrugged. "It's been done before, too many times. I prefer a different scene."

"If ever you change your mind I could

put you in touch with people who could supply you with a dozen plots," Slade offered, and smiled slowly as the grey eyes held his over a long, sardonic moment. "Just a thought."

The meal was almost over before Marie's name was mentioned. It was Ryan who brought it up with a thinly disguised deliberation which briefly widened the other man's lips.

"That one," he said, "has no need of a guardian. She chooses her own way."

"I'd already formed that opinion," Ryan came back without expression. "Just a matter of confirmation. She was disappointed not to be invited along with us."

"A neglect I will have to make up for." A look passed between the two men, then Slade pushed back his chair. "You'll excuse me for leaving you so abruptly," he said to Gina with an apologetic smile, "but I have an urgent appointment in Nassau. Forget about the boat—it's been taken care of. No need to rush away. Stay and finish your wine."

He was gone before she could find

anything to say. Disconcerted, she glanced at Ryan. "That was rather ill-mannered, wasn't it?"

"Indulgence over," he said with irritating calm. "It's back to business again now. If you've finished we may as well make tracks ourselves."

The same blue-suited Nassauvian appeared from nowhere to accompany them back down to the boat. He didn't speak at all this time, just stood at the end of the landing stage watching them put out.

"Is he some kind of bodyguard?" Gina asked dryly as they headed east. "He's enough to give anybody the shivers."

"Forget it," Ryan advised without taking his eyes from the perspex wind-deflector. "You're not likely to be seeing him again."

"That won't be any loss." She paused, waiting for him to say something else. When he didn't she added slowly, "I'm still not sure what all that was about."

"He wanted to size you up, see for himself just how big an error of judgment had been made. You came up with just the right image in that dress. It makes you look as shining innocent as you are."

"Not so innocent . . . now." Her voice was tight. "You took care of that."

"I took care of nothing. You got off light. And for God's sake shut up about it."

"Guilty conscience?" she queried silkily. "I'd have thought you were past that kind of weakness."

"I'm not past anything," he clipped back. "Right now . . ." He stopped, shook his head, expression suddenly weary. "Gina, do me a favour."

Her chin lifted. "Why should I?"

"For your own good."

"How thoughtful. What?"

"Let me put you on a plane for home before I leave. There's a London flight this evening. Time to get your tickets changed."

Her voice sounded small and far away. "I think you've done more than enough for me, thanks."

"You'll be on your own," he warned,

ignoring the sarcasm. "Your friend Marie has other interests."

"She's welcome to them. I can manage without her." She hurt inside. "Just go back to your solitude and leave me alone, will you."

"All right, if that's the way you want it." His tone was short. "I'm not going to apologise for what happened last night. You had it coming."

"So you keep telling me. You might some day convince yourself."

They didn't speak again. Watching the glittering coastline, Gina found she could barely see through the tears in her eyes. She wanted to crawl away somewhere like a wounded animal and hide, both from him and from herself.

# 6

MARIE left the hotel a couple of days later, Gina made no attempt to dissuade her from going, recognising the futility. If Slade Harley was what she had been looking for then good luck to her. She only hoped luck would be enough.

Her own small stock of traveller's cheques had dwindled at an alarming rate, despite all efforts to economise. Meals were so terribly expensive here in the hotel, and she had no means of transport to try finding anywhere cheaper. She doubted if such places existed anyway outside of the shanty-town area behind Nassau, and that was no place to go alone.

Not that she needed to have stayed alone had her inclination been otherwise. Eventually she took to sunbathing on her balcony in order to spare herself the necessity of discouraging would-be

176

companions. Marie had been wrong, she thought cynically on more than one occasion. She would have done far better on her own—although prospective husbands were probably in short supply.

Neil Davids turned up unexpectedly one night, coming on her in the lounge where she was trying to work out how she could afford to eat tonight.

"I was away longer than I anticipated," he said after initial greetings. "I suppose Marie got tired of waiting?"

Gina looked at him for a moment before answering, thinking that Marie would have done far better to wait and see what this man might have offered her.

"You haven't seen Ryan?" she asked carefully.

"No. I only got back this afternoon." He sounded surprised. "He's been over here?"

"Yes." She saw no reason to go into the whole story. Let Ryan do the telling himself. No doubt he would make a book of it. "Marie isn't staying here any longer," she said.

"Oh." His brows lifted. "Where did she go?"

"Do you know of a man called Slade Harley?"

A shadow passed across Neil's face. "She didn't?"

"I'm afraid so."

"The damned fool! She'll . . ." He broke off abruptly, sat still for a moment, then shrugged his shoulders. "Well, that's her look-out. She knew what she was doing." His eyes came back to Gina, taking on a new expression. "How the devil did a girl like you come to get mixed up with someone like her anyway?"

Back to square one, she thought. She only wished she could be. "It's a long story," she shrugged.

"Then tell it to me over dinner."

Her face tautened. "I don't think so, thanks."

He studied her a moment, then laughed. "Not with any ulterior motives, Gina. There are women and women. Some you use, some you cherish. I need company, that's all—intelligent company wrapped up in a delightful packaging for preference. You haven't already eaten?"

"No," she admitted.

"Then please do me the favour."

She capitulated eventually, for the very good reason that she had eaten little since breakfast and could barely afford to sample even the cheapest selection from the menu in the dining room. The beach snack bar was keeping her going, although she hated junk food. However, that was long closed.

Seated across from Neil at a table on the terrace, she thought of that first night and felt an iron hand close about her chest. It seemed such a long time ago; another lifetime. What a little fool she had been!

"You're different, you know," Neil said suddenly after he had ordered. "A fortnight ago you sat there with stars in your eyes, tonight you look . . ." He paused, shook his head. "I'm not sure what it is, but something's gone."

"Illusion," she said. "I realised things aren't always what they seemed."

"True, but it's a pity you had to learn

that this way. Obviously you didn't know Marie very well?"

"No, I didn't." She was quite prepared to let him believe she had been referring to Marie's defection. "I took her at face value."

He smiled a little. "That's one way of putting it. Did you say Ryan had been over?"

She stiffened involuntarily. "Yes."

"To see you?"

Gina attempted a laugh. "I wouldn't put it that way."

"Then which way would you put it? Or is that another long story?"

She sighed. "It's all part and parcel, and I don't think I want to tell it. Do you mind? You can get it all from Ryan himself when you see him."

"Want to bet? That man's the biggest clam alive unless he wants you to know something." He paused. "Might he want me to know this?"

"There's every chance."

It was Neil's turn to sigh. "Talking of clams, you don't do a bad job yourself.

Okay, I'll leave it alone. Whatever went off between you two, it's your affair."

Not quite, she wanted to say. That wasn't in the plan.

She wondered if Neil realised just what kind of a louse his friend could be. And if he did, would he consider it such a bad trait? Men stuck together.

"Having a good time?" asked the all-too-familiar voice, jerking her out of her thoughts and back into a world which had suddenly acquired a totally new low. Ryan stood there at the side of the table, dressed as he had been that first night in tuxedo and dark trousers, the smile on his face as hard as nails. "I went out to the house," he added to Neil. "They told me you'd come down here. Looking for Marie?"

"Well, yes." The older man looked momentarily disconcerted, as if taken aback by the other's tone. "Sit down, man. What brought you across in the middle of the week?"

"I put my MS in the post this afternoon." Ryan took one of the free seats, pulling it round so that he faced

Gina at an angle. His eyes were sardonic. "Standing in?"

"Gina agreed to have dinner with me after a hint of persuasion on my part," Neil chipped in before she could answer. "She's already told me about Marie."

"What about Marie?"

"I told Neil where she was and who with," Gina returned evenly. "He took the disappointment like the gentleman he is."

Neil laughed. "It's been a long time since anybody called me one of those! I'll try to live up to it."

"Not this time round, you won't," said Ryan, and drew a sudden frown from the other man.

"Now wait a minute! Don't get the wrong idea. I don't have designs on Gina."

"No?" The word held a wealth of irony. "I've known you a long time, remember."

"When you've both finished," said Gina with satire, "I think I might have a say in whom I choose to dine with." She looked at Ryan with dislike written quite plainly in her eyes, ignoring the inevitable leap of her pulses because that was simply chemistry and impossible to cancel out whatever the circumstances. "For someone who's just arrived you take a whole lot on yourself!"

"I could take a whole lot more," he said. "I suppose you've dined out most nights since I left."

"Oh, but of course. They've been picking me up in droves!" She shrugged at the tautening of his expression. "What does it matter to you? You're not my keeper."

"I'm beginning to feel distinctly *de trop* here," put in Neil on a rueful note. "Gina, please believe I had no intention of trying to make this anything more than a pleasant evening."

"I do." She smiled at him with a purposeful warmth. "You see, I trust my instincts, and they tell me you're not half the rake some people make you out to be—at least, not where I'm concerned. Disregarding the interruption, where . . ." Ryan put a hand under her elbow and stood up, drawing her with him. "I want to talk to you," he said. "We'll do it on the dance floor."

"Don't mind me," Neil said plaintively. "I'm only the host."

Gina went with him because she didn't intend giving him the pleasure of making her go by force. On the floor he pulled her hardily towards him and held her there, hands burning a hole through the fine material of her dress.

"What are you trying to prove?" he demanded, low-toned. "Neil Davids is twenty years older than you."

"And you're eleven." She gave a cracked little laugh. "Underline that!"

His jaw contracted shortly. "Cut out the wisecracks, I'm not in the mood."

"Neither am I in the mood!" She said it viciously. "Not for any of this. I thought I'd seen the last of you!"

"Like the proverbial bad penny I keep turning up."

"To save me from myself?"

His arms tightened their hold. "I came looking for Neil."

"To save him from himself, then. Don't

you think he's old enough to make his own decisions?"

"Not this time."

"That's *my* decision."

"Stop it, damn you!" He sounded suddenly at the end of his tether. "Gina, don't be like this. It isn't you."

"How would you know what I'm like? Really like, I mean. You saw the side of me you wanted to see, the side you wanted to flatten. Well, all right, so you flattened it—right out of existence. This is what's left."

Ryan stopped moving and looked down at her for a moment, ignoring the curious glances they were attracting from those about them. Then he stepped away from her and took her hand, leading her through the dancers to the far terrace doors and out into the night.

They were cut off from the tables down here by a trellis covered in red jasmine, the steps on the right landing down to the gardens. He didn't take her far, only into the shadows of the nearest trees, pulling her round in front of him and holding her there with his fingers still locked about her wrist.

"Isn't this about where we came in?" she asked brightly. "I hate repeat performances!"

She got one anyway, only this time with the difference that she was expecting it and could therefore control her reactions. When Ryan finally lifted his head his expression held a peculiar quality.

"I did an excellent job, didn't I?" he said.

"Where you're concerned, yes. On the other hand, I learned quite a lot about lovemaking in general which might stand me in good stead some day. I suppose I should thank you for that. After all, your services usually come at a premium!"

"Stop it, Gina." He said it quite gently, surprising her into silence for a moment. "All right, so I went too far with you. If it's any consolation, I've been kicking myself ever since."

"Good. That saves me the trouble of doing it for you."

"I'm trying to apologise."

186

"I don't want your apologies!"

"Then what do you want?"

"Nothing. Nothing you can give me." Her voice sounded cracked. "Just take me back to Neil. It's heaven to be with someone civilised again."

A muscle jerked alongside his mouth. "That's the kind of thing that got you put down last time. Would you like another sample?"

"You just tried that."

"I didn't *try* anything. The ice maiden act only works so far."

"It isn't an act." Her limbs were trembling and she couldn't stop them. "That's the way you make me feel inside. I daresay you could gain some kind of reaction if you put your mind to it—you're an expert at knowing where and how to touch. But then you've had so much practice, haven't you?"

It was a moment before he moved or spoke. All expression had been wiped from his face.

"When do you go home?" he asked at last on a hard note.

"The day after tomorrow," she said.

"It's the best place for you. All right, I'll take you back to Neil."

He walked at her side, he even took her arm when they mounted steps, but it was like being with a total stranger. Neil was sitting where they had left him. He watched them coming with a curious expression.

"I ordered drinks," he said. "Wasn't sure when we might get round to eating."

Ryan saw Gina into her seat but remained standing himself. "I have to go," he said. "I'll see you at the weekend, Neil."

The other's brows lifted. "You're going back to the island tonight?"

"No, I'm going fishing for a couple of days." Ryan's glance down at Gina held hard mockery. "Have a pleasant flight home."

She curled her hand around her glass as he left, feeling Neil's eyes on her but unable to bring herself to meet them right away.

"Far be it from me to ask what all that

was about," he said, "but what was all that about?"

"Nothing." Her voice was thick.

"Oh, come on. Tell me to mind my own business, or even to get lost, but don't expect me to believe that." He paused meaningfully. "Has Ryan been doing something he shouldn't?"

She had to smile a little at the deliberate use of the archaic term. "I'm not breaking my heart over him, if that's what you mean. I'm not one of his conquests." Neither was she, she reflected hardily. Only physically, and that didn't count. She felt cold inside, just as she had told him; as if nothing or no one would ever warm her again. "He just can't take rejection," she added with a hint of malice.

"Shouldn't think he's had much practice," Neil agreed. "Women tend to fall into his arms with monotonous willingness. It does my heart good to know he's fallible."

She looked at him then. "I thought you were friends?"

"So we are. He has two distinct advantages—age and mobility."

"Mobility may be one, I'd switch the other around."

His eyes crinkled. "You prefer a man old enough to be your father rather than your brother, is that what you're saying? You know, if I didn't know better, I might believe you were making a pass at me."

"Is that so impossible?" she asked lightly.

"Unlikely. I'd say you'd had more than enough of male chauvinism this time round."

She smiled. "You don't strike me as being at all chauvinistic."

"Oh, but I am. We all are basically—vainglorious, and complacent with it. A woman pays homage or makes way for one who will. Obviously you sold Ryan short."

"Obviously." Her smile felt stiff. "Would you mind if we talked about something else?"

"Not one bit. Tell me about yourself away from this place."

It was gone eleven when they finally left the restaurant.

"How about tomorrow?" Neil asked out in the lobby. "I'd like to take you into town and give you a real evening out Nassau style."

"I don't think so," Gina said evenly. "Thanks all the same, Neil, but I'll be off early the next morning."

"You're probably wise," he came back wryly. "I'm not sure how long my better instincts would last. You're an unsual and very lovely young woman, Gina. I envy the man who finally gets you."

If she ever decided to get got at all, she reflected unemotionally up in her room. It would be a long time before she felt like any kind of intimate acquaintance with a man again.

She arrived back in England at eight o'clock on a clear blue October morning to find a real autumn nip in the air. Marie's defection was a nine-day wonder at the office and then forgotten in the rush of work preceding Christmas. Gradually the whole holiday fiasco took on a dreamlike quality in Gina's mind. Had she really ever been to the Bahamas, had she ever really met Ryan Barras—or was it all a figment of her imagination?

She spent Christmas day with her landlady's family, grateful for the invitation in a way which only those with nowhere else to go can be. The Robinsons had two sons and a daughter, the latter, Shirley, still being at school. Chris, the eldest son at twenty-six, was a Second Officer in the Merchant Navy, and the apple of his mother's eye. A blond six-footer with an engaging grin and a cheerful disposition, he struck Gina favourably from the very first moment of introduction.

"I saw you coming in and out once or twice last time I was home on leave," he told her. "Just moved here then, hadn't you?"

"Yes," she said. "I was sharing a flat with two other girls before this, but it didn't really work out."

"Shouldn't imagine it would. I know

what it's like bunking in with a load of others."

"I thought officers would have their own cabins," she said with a smile.

"They do. I came up the hard way."

"He wanted to go in the Navy since he was eight," his mother said fondly. "I always thought he meant the Royal Navy."

"Too much discipline," he grinned. "And not enough pay. Did I tell you I'd put in for a transfer to the Line's cruise ships? There's a vacancy for a Number Two on the *Enterprise*."

"To boldly go where no man has gone before," quoted his younger brother Andrew promptly. "You'd think they'd come up with some original names, wouldn't you!"

"She was named before that series started," Chris retorted, and drew a snort.

"Must be ready for the scrapyard, then!"

"No, she isn't. She just had a complete refit. She's doing five different three-week Med runs this summer. I rather fancy myself entertaining a shipload of young lovelies!"

Gina was laughing. "I think you'd do it very well too. I can see you now pacing the deck in sparkling white with your hat set at a rakish angle!"

"Cap," he corrected, laughing with her. "And they're to be worn straight at all times, more's the pity!" He looked at her for a moment, obviously appreciating her appearance in the long-sleeved red dress she had thought appropriate to the occasion. "If I get the job you'll have to take a cruise with us."

"I'll think about it," she promised.

Later, finding herself sitting next to him in the midst of a family party gathering which threatened to overflow even the large ground-floor apartment, she said, "You're really counting on this transfer, aren't you, Chris?"

"Yes, I am," he admitted. "Cruising's the cream in the doughnut. Do you blame me?"

"Not a bit. Do you stand a good chance?"

"So I'm told." The irrepressible grin widened his lips.

"I'm the type they need to keep all the girls happy."

"Big, blond and beautiful," Gina murmured dutifully. "They'll have to use you in the advertising campaign: See the Med with Christopher Robinson!"

"Don't you start," he groaned. "I've had to put up with leg-pulling since I was in nursery school!"

It was a moment before his meaning sank in. "Oh, I see," she said. "I'm afraid it hadn't struck me."

"If you'd been asked where Winnie was as many times as I have you'd be as sensitive," on a rueful note. "I wouldn't even look at a teddy bear when I was a kid."

"Somebody has to be the butt," said Gina, "or what would all the comedians do?"

Brown eyes regarded her thoughtfully. "You're a bit of a cynic, aren't you?" he commented. "Natural or acquired?"

Acquired, she could have told him, oh

very definitely acquired. For a fleeting moment she wondered what Ryan was doing now—and could hazard a guess. She smiled and said lightly, "Just one of my many guises."

"I'd like to get to know the rest." His tone was suddenly serious. "You're different, Gina." He paused. "What are you doing tomorrow?"

"Not a lot," she admitted.

"Then how about coming to the match with me, then on somewhere for the evening?"

"I'd like that," she said, and meant it.

"Great." He sounded jubilant. "It's a date!"

Knowing little about the rules of football, Gina nevertheless enjoyed that Boxing Day game. Standing in the cold air with Chris's arm casually about her shoulders as they cheered on his team, she felt the underlying depression of the last few weeks lift.

They went back to the house to change before going up West for what Chris termed a night on the town. Dining with him, dancing with him, Gina closed her mind to the inevitable comparisons and concentrated on enjoying his company. It wasn't difficult because he was good company. They did a lot of laughing together, and talking. She felt easy with him.

The whole ground floor of the house was in darkness when they eventually got back to Ealing. Gina invited him up to her first floor flatlet for coffee, smiling as she switched on a couple of lamps in the little sitting room.

"It seems strange somehow, inviting you into your own house."

"Except that it isn't. Not this part of it." He glanced around. "You've made it very comfortable. Good idea having the bed fold up into the wall like that, wasn't it?"

"Yours?" she asked, and he made at her a sweeping bow.

"Just one of my many guises."

Later, when he kissed her goodnight, it was with a warmth she found both comforting and appealing. This was what she wanted, a nice friendly relationship which made no deep emotional demands.

It didn't stay that way, of course—at least not wholly. They spent a great deal of that leave together, and Gina found herself missing him when he rejoined his ship. His letters came regularly over the following weeks, long and chatty, full of descriptions of places he had seen, things he had done. There was also a hint of something else, a growing intimacy she could not ignore. Uncertain of her own feelings, she tried to keep the tone of her replies on a purely friendly level, but it was difficult not to respond to the knowledge of being wanted emotionally as well as physically by someone.

Meanwhile, she had gained promotion in her job, dealing more with people and less with pure paper work. Several times she found herself roped in to help provide organised entertainment for some client, and was gratified to realise she could cope quite comfortably with most situations. She described one incident in a letter to Chris regarding an Arab sheik's invitation to have her join his band of wives with humour. "They're only allowed four at any one time," she wrote. "so he would have had to divorce one of his present ones to fit me in, poor woman! Needless to say, I regretfully declined." To her surprise, Chris wrote back on an angry note telling her to pack the job in before some damned Arab decided not to ask first. Gina ignored the advice but made a point of not talking about her job from then on.

Chris's next leave towards the middle of March found their relationship on a different footing. His transfer had come through, and he was all set to join his new ship after this leave ready for the summer schedule. He had enough service behind him to have reached the stage at which he was allowed to take along certain specified members of his immediate family on the occasional voyage, and made it plain to Gina that he had this idea in mind for them on a husband and wife basis in the not too distant future. Fond of him as she undoubtedly was, Gina refused to commit herself, but it was obvious by the time he went to join his ship that he was taking it for granted they would be getting engaged the next time he came home in July.

Often over the following few weeks, Gina wondered why she hesitated. Chris was all any girl could ask in the way of a husband, and he loved her. She got on exceptionally well with his family and knew they approved of the match. So what was wrong with her?

She was at her desk one bright April morning sorting through some stills for an anti-smoking campaign when her boss Hugh Fisher came to the door of his inner sanctum. He was wearing a rather odd expression, she thought, but there was nothing so unusual in his request.

"Got a client's client just in from the States who needs somebody to take him out to dinner and provide a little congenial company tonight," he said. "How about it?" Gina smiled. "Sometimes I think you're running an escort service here on the side."

"Sometimes I agree with you," he came back sourly. "Will you do it?"

"Why not? I'm not doing anything else, and a free night out on the town isn't to be sneezed at. Who is he?"

"A writer. Name of—" he peered at a slip of paper he held—"Sam Brownlow."

"Never heard of him," she said, and drew another sour smile.

"We haven't started promoting him yet."

"Who's he publishing with?" Gina asked, interested. "In England, I mean."

"I've got it down somewhere. Can't remember off-hand." He consulted the bit of paper again. "You're to pick him up at his hotel at eight. He'll take care of the arrangements."

"Sounds as if he knows his way around," she commented. "You'd think he could find his own company."

"He doesn't know anybody over here, apparently. No place lonelier than a big city when you're on your own."

Gina could go along with that. Walking through the crowded streets she often felt that if she fell down dead people would simply walk around her. Being taken into

Chris's family the way she had gave her a feeling of belonging somewhere. She had a base, and people who cared about her. Added to a job she liked and which was reasonably well paid, it amounted to a whole lot.

"Which hotel?" she asked.

"The Hilton."

Her brows lifted. "He must be good!"

"Brilliant." The tone was dry. "Or so I'm told. Eight o'clock—I'll confirm that."

One of Gina's male colleagues came to a stop at her desk as Hugh went back into his office.

"I've two tickcts for *Evita* tonight," he said. "Surprise present from a grateful client. Fancy coming with me?"

She shook her head regretfully. "I wish you'd asked me earlier. I'd love to see that show, but I'm afraid I'm already booked."

"Your sailor boy-friend home from sea again?" he asked.

"No, I'm wining and dining a writer."

"His expense sheet or ours?"

"I've no idea—Hugh didn't say. His, I

should think. It was his own idea, apparently."

"Wonder how he knew we'd anyone available?"

"I don't suppose he did. We're doing the promotion, though, so I imagine we were the best bet."

"What about his publishers?"

"How would I know? Hugh doesn't go in for detail."

"You're telling me? I suppose you do know his name." She told him, receiving a blank shake of his head in reply. "Never heard of the man."

That made two of them, Gina reflected dryly as he departed. It hadn't occurred to her to ask Hugh what the man had written. No doubt he wouldn't remember that either. Her boss spent his life referring to bits of paper on which he scribbled countless messages, yet nobody could say he didn't do his job. Now she thought of it, it was unusual for the request to have come directly from the author himself when normally his agent or his British publishers would be organising his entertainment—especially if he was important enough to be put up at the Hilton. However, hers not to reason why. She only hoped he would be congenial company and not too self-obsessed. She had no objections to talking about his work all night but didn't fancy hearing his life story from A to Z. She left the office early in order to have plenty of time to change and get back into town for eight. It had been showering on and off all day, but seemed to have settled down at last to a steady stream of sunshine for the final few hours. Missing the rush hour made the tube ride almost pleasant. She would order a taxi back, she decided. She hated riding on the tube in a long dress, and anyway she could claim the expense from Hugh tomorrow. She smiled to herself at the thought of his response. Hugh Fisher liked to play the tough boss, but he was really a darling with a heart of gold underneath the gruff exterior.

Mrs. Robinson came to her front door as Gina let herself into the hall. "There's a letter for you from Chris," she announced. "I put it in your box. I had one too."

"Oh, that's good." Gina was relieved. Chris's mother tended to get just a little upset when her son neglected to send her a weekly letter along with the one he sent Gina. Understandable, she supposed. She was apparently the first girl Chris had ever been really serious about, and although his mother liked her and they got along pretty well, there was no getting away from the fact that her days of counting this as his home would be numbered if they did decide to get married. About that Gina still couldn't make up her mind. She thought so much of Chris, but was it enough? Marriage wasn't something one stepped into lightly. She had to be sure.

"There's that documentary you wanted to watch on tonight," Mrs. Robinson added. "Andrew's going out, so you might get some peace if you want to come down."

"I wish I could," Gina said for the second time that day, "but I have to go out tonight. Business," she felt impelled to add, seeing the faint light of suspicion in the other eyes. She was sure Mrs. Robinson didn't mean to keep an eye on her in that sense, but she would certainly have wondered why had any attempt been made to keep the nature of her date a secret. "I'm taking an author out to dinner."

"A man?" came the doubtful reply, and Gina hid a smile.

"Well, yes, as a matter of fact."

"He's not another Arab, is he?"

This time the smile could not be kept back. "No, he isn't an Arab. He's American—I think. At least that's where he comes from."

"Elderly?"

"I don't know." Until that moment Gina hadn't thought about it. "I shouldn't think so. He's an unknown—over here at any rate." She added gently, "It's all right, really, Mrs. Robinson. I'll be telling Chris all about it. I must go now or I won't have time to read his letter properly."

The envelope was postmarked Tangier a week ago. By now he would be at the other end of the Mediterranean and halfway through his first seasonal voyage as Second Officer Robinson of the *Enterprise*. From the tone of his letters he certainly seemed to be enjoying life. He had his own table at dinner and was allowed to choose those he wished to invite to share a meal together on certain nights of the week. "If you only knew the golden opportunities I've turned down since we left Southampton," he wrote. "The minute you get into whites it acts like an aphrodisiac on the girls aboard! Officers are expected to help entertain the passengers yet keep their cool at all times and not get involved. If I didn't have you to think about I might find that rule a bit difficult to stick to. Some don't make any attempt. The Number Three even runs a book on how long it will take to get to various stages with the best looking girls on board. I won't detail them—the stages, I mean—but Number Five gets an invite to a cabin, and he's made it three times already this trip. We all know what they say about sailors having a girl in every port, but this is ridiculous!"

Methinks the gentleman protests too much, Gina thought a little dryly, putting the letter down. So far as she was concerned, Chris was still free to indulge whatever fancies took him. This change of job might be what they both needed to test the strength of their feelings for one another. If he were starting already to feel tied down then it wouldn't work out. It couldn't.

She booked a taxi over the phone to pick her up at seven-thirty, then took a look through her wardrobe for something to wear. For the Hilton it had to look good, although she didn't suppose they would be eating there. Finally she settled on a silver-grey crêpe she had bought in the Christmas sales for a song because it was shopsoiled. Cleaned, it had come up beautifully. It had narrow shoe-string straps over the shoulders and its own matching jacket fitted to the waist. Chris thought she looked smashing in it but considered it a waste of money for the times she would be able to wear it. Well, this was one now and she was glad of it. Teamed with silver sandals and the plaited silver necklet he had brought her back from his last voyage, it looked just great.

Her hair had grown these last months. She wore it now in a bell shape on a level with her chin, a style which made her eyes look longer—or so she had been told. She used a smear of blue shadow on each lid, and finished off with the minimum of mascara, thankful that her lashes and brows were darker than her hair. The latter had retained some of the silvery lights created by the sun, lying smooth and glossy about her face. The changes in her went deeper than the merely obvious, though. She had both gained and lost something intrinsic to her former self.

The taxi arrived promptly, and the traffic into town was light. By five minutes to the hour she was walking in through the big glass doors fronting the hotel. The receptionist gave her a curiously speculative look when she asked for Mr. Brownlow.

"Oh yes," he said, "would you go right up to the suite." A suite! At the Hilton! Gina gave herself a mental shake. Hers not to reason why, remember. She found herself anticipating this meeting with a new interest. Who on earth was Sam Brownlow?

She took the lift to the appropriate floor, stepping out onto sumptuously thick carpeting. There was no one else about as she knocked tentatively on the door. No one to see the blood drain suddenly from her face when it opened except the man standing there looking at her.

"Hallo, Gina," he said.

# 7

SHOCK kept her motionless for a brief suspended moment. When she turned it was blindly, with no other thought in mind but to get away. But Ryan was swifter, shooting out a hand to grasp her arm and draw her into the room, then closing the door and leaning against it so that she had no escape.

He looked just the same, she thought painfully. Arrogant, sure of himself—sure of her too. Well, that was something she could handle for a start.

"I might have known when Hugh said the Hilton," she brought out coldly. "Is he in on this too?"

"He'd have to be, wouldn't he?" His tone was dry. "Not that he didn't take some persuading to play along. Luckily we're personally acquainted. It makes a difference."

"What did you tell him?" she demanded.

He shrugged easily. " Just that we met in the Bahamas a few months ago and I wanted to surprise you."

"All right, so you surprised me. Now I'd like to leave, please."

"Why?" he asked. "Scared?"

"Of you?" She looked him up and down with deliberation, closing her mind to his lean attraction in the white silk shirt and silver-grey trousers that were almost a match for her dress. "I got over that a long time ago."

"Then you don't have anything to worry about." He indicated the luxurious sitting room behind her. "Come and have a drink before we leave. I thought we might have dinner then take in a nightclub. Glad you came dressed for it."

"I don't want a drink," she said, "and I'm not going anywhere with you."

His brows lifted. "It's part of your job."

"Only if I agree to do it."

"You did agree to do it. Hugh rang me back to tell me so."

"Because I thought you were someone else."

"I'm still a client," he pointed out.

"Not directly. Your publishing house pays the bills."

"That's splitting hairs. I'm sure Hugh would agree with me. Keep the clients sweet, we need 'em."

"There are other accounts far larger and more important."

"I'll inform my publishers. They'll go a bundle on being told their stuff is unimportant."

"That wasn't what I said."

"It's what you implied. Just remember there are other promotion firms too."

Gina gazed at him for a long moment, breathing hard. "You're threatening me, aren't you?" she said. "Either I go along with what you want or you persuade your publishers to put their business with someone else. Do you really think you're that important?"

"To them, yes. There aren't that many world class best-sellers to go around."

"Modesty isn't your strong point, is it?" she said bitingly, and drew a faint smile.

"False modesty, no. I only write one book a year, which means my name needs to be kept in the public eye between times. They're a fickle lot without an occasional sop to the collective imagination. My readers like to think of me as an extension of some of my heroes, so that's what we give them."

"But none of it's really true, is that what you're telling me?" There was irony in her voice. "You never indulged in any of those affairs so widely reported!"

"I wouldn't say never, just not as often. I don't have that amount of stamina."

"How sad!"

He laughed unexpectedly. "If you think you'll get me mad enough to tell you to get out of here you've another think coming."

"Why?" she said passionately. "Just tell me why!"

"Because I wanted to see you again." He studied her appraisiugly. "You look different. Not just your hair, something else."

"I grew up," she said. "Better late than never. I've a lot to thank you for."

"I was a louse," he agreed "It's haunted me ever since. That's why I needed to see you again, to tell you so." He paused fleetingly. "That night I came to the hotel I really came looking for you, not Neil. I wanted to straighten things out before you came back home. Finding you with him was . . . well, I'm afraid I jumped to conclusions."

"You made that rather obvious," Gina got out, recalling the expression on his face when she had glanced up and seen him standing there.

"And then your attitude," he went on as if she hadn't spoken. "You resented being taken away from him."

"The way you did it I should think I did! Neil had been kind enough to ask me to have dinner with him. There were no strings attached. Then you turn up and start laying down the law as though you had some personal responsibility for me!"

"That was the way I felt. I was the one who'd left you there with very little money. I should have insisted on putting you on that plane for home."

"Except that nothing on earth would have persuaded me to borrow money from you," she retorted bitterly. "I don't see the point in going into all of it again. Why did you really set this up, Ryan?"

"I told you, I had to see you again."

"You mean you were bored and thought I might provide you with a little easy entertainment?" Her laugh was brittle. "I'm afraid you're right out of luck. My fiancé might object."

Something flickered in the grey eyes. "I don't see any ring."

"We're waiting until his next leave. He's a cruise ship officer—they're in the Med at the moment."

"I see. Congratulations." He sounded genuine about it, the smile holding no hint of irony. "He wouldn't object to a purely platonic dinner, would he?"

"Not if it was."

Dark brows lifted. "You mean it wouldn't be for you?" He smiled again at the look on her face. "Gina, I promise you,

I've no designs on you this time round. I wanted to put things right, and I knew you'd refuse to see me if I contacted you in any normal way."

Gazing at him she felt suddenly rather foolish. Why had she taken it for granted that his interest in her should be of the physical variety? His explanation was plausible enough. He simply wanted to clear his conscience over an incident of which he was basically ashamed. He was right about her refusing to have seen him had he approached her through normal channels. This had been the only way. She should feel flattered that he should go to so much trouble to try to put things right between them. Some men would just have said to hell with it.

"It seems you're not the only one to jump to false conclusions," she said wryly. "You left me with a very suspicious mind, that's all."

"Not surprisingly. I took a mean advantage for totally inadequate reasons, then added insult to injury by believing you had something going with Neil that night at the hotel." He paused a moment, then slowly held out his hand. "Friends?"

Gina took it only a little hesitantly, feeling the firm warmth act like a trigger on her memory. "Friends," she said.

"Fine. Now about dinner?"

If she refused now, Gina reflected, it would intimate that she was still attaching more importance to the invitation than existed. Chris wouldn't be keen on the idea regardless of circumstances, but what could she do? "All right," she agreed. "Seeing that I'm already here."

"Then let's have that drink. The table is reserved for nine. It won't take more than a few minutes by cab. What will you have?"

"Sherry, please. Medium dry." She took a seat on the low chesterfield and watched him move to the drinks tray already set out on a table a short distance away, registering the superb fit of the silk shirt across his shoulders, the long powerful line of his legs sensed rather than seen beneath the fine grey cloth. Her pet hate was a man in trousers which sagged in the seat. These didn't. They fitted the way they should, moulding the firm muscularity in a manner which brought back a vivid mental picture of him standing naked on the beach down by the lagoon that evening. Difficult now to believe it had all really happened.

"Would you say you spent more time in the States than anywhere else overall?" she asked on a casual note.

"I guess so," he said. He brought the drinks across, handing her glass to her with a quizzical look. "Why?"

"Just a thought. You don't have an American accent exactly, but your phrasing sometimes swings that way."

He smiled. "It's a habit easily picked up. When I was in Australia researching *Thicker Than Water* I acquired one or two Aussie phrases too. My father would have thrown a true blue fit if he'd ever heard me!"

"Very pro-British, was he?"

"To the point of being anti-everywhere else. He never travelled outside the country if he could avoid it, and treated all foreigners like morons. He was a wizard on the stock market, though. One of the Exchange's most revered members." He was sitting beside her now on the chesterfield, not too close, voice easy and relaxed. "I was only twenty when he died. He went the way he would have wanted to, at his desk with a cigar between his lips and his finger on the pulse."

"And your mother?" Gina asked, trying not to sound too vitally interested.

"Killed in a car crash when I was twelve."

"That's the way my father died," she said. "Only I was much younger than that. I can barely remember him at all."

"It must have been difficult for your mother bringing up a child on her own."

"I don't think it was too bad financially. Apparently he'd been well insured."

"She can't have been that old. Didn't she ever consider marrying again?"

Gina smiled a little. "I think she was a one-man woman. Once or twice I thought it was going to happen, but it always fell through."

"For your sake, perhaps."

"Oh, no, I'd have loved a father. Then I'd have been like all the other girls at school."

"Was it so important to be like everyone else?"

"To a child it's usually all-important. I even went to the length of telling some of my school friends that my father wasn't really dead at all, but a Secret Service agent away on a mission. Only one of them told her mother and she told mine, so that story didn't last long."

Ryan was smiling. "Sounds as if you had a vivid imagination. Never think of taking up writing as a career?"

She laughed. "I once got as far as page two of an adventure story for girls titled *The Mystery of The Ring*, but I ran out of ideas after they'd found the ring and discovered that the original owner had met with a ghastly death."

"If all that happened by page two I'm not surprised!"

"Well, at nine you don't hang around building up suspense." She paused, looking at him. "Did writing come naturally to you?"

"I suppose it must have done," with a shrug. "My first novel was accepted as it stood."

"That was the one set in Jamaica, wasn't it?"

"That's right. I lived there for a year while that book took shape in my mind until in the end I had to commit it to paper just to get it out of my system."

They talked easily for another quarter of an hour or so before Ryan glanced at the time.

"May as well be making a move," he said. "I hope you like Greek food?"

"I've never really tried any," she admitted. "Unless you can count home-made moussaka?"

"I doubt if Stavros would count it as anything but fit for the dustbin. Anyway, you can try the real stuff and see how it compares."

Gina was completely relaxed by the time they reached the restaurant. Short of any ulterior motivation, Ryan was superb company. Resolutely she ignored the tiny area of depression hovering on the edge of her mind, plus the reason for it being there at all. Having a man like Ryan Barras as a friend could only be a good thing when she knew how impossible it would have been to handle the alternative—had it been offered. Chris could raise no objection to this. After all, he wasn't exactly living a monk's life himself.

The restaurant was one she had heard of but regarded as far beyond her pocket. Ryan was obviously well known, for he was greeted by name and led to a secluded table on the upper floor. Looking round her, Gina wondered who he had last brought here to ply with food and wine at the start of an evening. Her circumstances were different, of course, as this was the whole extent of the evening.

She chose kebabs in preference to the moussaka, and thoroughly enjoyed the tender, succulent pieces of lamb skewered between slivers of onion, mushroom and pepper and served on a bed of rice. For dessert she ate fresh fruit salad and cream, and elected to try the Turkish coffee, finding the latter too thick and sweet for her taste.

"Nothing ventured, nothing gained," she said in answer to Ryan's commiseration. "If I ever come here again I'll know to stick to the ordinary stuff. I enjoyed the rest anyway. It was delicious!"

"I'll tell Stavros. He'll be pleased to have a convert." He added easily, "You must have had kebabs before this, though."

"Not tasting the way those tasted."

"That's the marinating before the meat is cooked. A secret recipe. Would you like a brandy?"

"No, thanks, nothing else." She met his eyes, feeling the familiar tensing of muscle down in the pit of her stomach without surprise. Attraction didn't die as easily as that. She supposed it would always be there in one form or another whenever she thought of him. "It's been a lovely evening," she added.

"Does it have to be over?" he asked on the same casual note. "It's barely ten-thirty, and it is Friday night. You don't have to go into the office in the morning, do you?"

"Not this week. Sometimes it's necessary." She hesitated, aware that she too didn't want the evening to end yet reluctant to put her own basic reflexes to any further test. "I really think I should go home."

"Because of your fiancé? I don't imagine he's likely to be hitting the hay too early."

"He goes on watch at midnight," Gina came back on a slightly defensive note. "It doesn't give him too much opportunity for living it up with the passengers."

One dark brow rose a fraction. "Did I suggest he might be doing that?"

"Not exactly, but . . ."

"But the thought's there." He smiled a little. "You should learn to trust more. If you're going to marry the man you'll have to trust him—unless he's prepared to give up his job and stay at home with you."

"No, he isn't, and neither would I ask him to. And I do trust him!"

"Then you don't have anything to worry

about. Neither does he. That's settled, then. We'll go on somewhere. I won't keep you out too late."

No, Gina thought, he wouldn't. Mrs. Robinson would be listening for her coming in and she had no intention of trying to explain away a three o'clock return when she saw her again tomorrow. Living where she did wasn't exactly ideal, she acknowledged with a faint inward sigh, yet Chris was hardly going to understand if she started looking for another flat. And where would she find another she could afford? The only way was to share again, and that had to be a very last resort.

It was a warm night for the time of the year. Outside, Ryan suggested they walk for a while.

"It isn't so far to where we're going," he said, "but if you get tired say so and we'll get a cab—I mean a taxi."

She laughed with him, thinking how wonderful it was to have no aggression between them. Yet some small part of her missed it too, though she could not have explained exactly why. "I wasn't criticising you before," she said. "You're entitled to use whichever word comes easiest to you."

"Not every time." Under street lighting his smile seemed edged with something other than humour, an illusion swiftly dispelled when he widened it. "But I'll bear the advice in mind."

He took her hand when they crossed the road a little further along, retaining it casually on the far side, fingers lightly clasping hers in a gesture she could hardly misconstrue. To show that she did not misconstrue it she made no attempt to disengage, but was aware of a spreading of the ache deep within her.

From outside, their destination looked like any other building on the road with a graceful flight of iron railed steps leading up to a solid, brass-furnished front door. Inside, at a large mahogany desk set to the rear of the wide hallway, sat a lone man wearing evening dress.

"Mr. Barras!" he exclaimed with obvious and, Gina thought, unassumed pleasure. "We don't usually see you here this time of year!"

"Thought it was time I changed my habits," came the easy response. "Gina, meet Charles. Miss Tierson hasn't been here before, Charles."

"I'm sure not, or I would have remembered." A pair of bland eyes met Gina's. "Welcome to the Conley Club, Miss Tierson." As he spoke he was turning the large open book on the desk in front of him round and handing Ryan a pen. "I hope this will be the first of many visits."

Gina murmured some appropriate reply, and watched Ryan sign his own name, then write hers underneath and put the letter G at the side of it. Obviously this was a private club for members and guests of members only. But what kind of club?

"Don't look so worried," Ryan advised on an amused note as they descended a staircase to the lower regions from where filtered the sound of music. "You won't find any orgies here. Ronald Conley runs

228

the place strictly according to the book. His hostesses are here to dance with and generally entertain the lonely by listening to their woes, but nothing more than that. There isn't even a strip show."

"Then why the private licence?" Gina asked, determined not to reveal any embarrassment over his accurate reading of her thoughts.

"Gaming rooms," was the succinct reply. He gave the girl in the cloakroom booth at the foot of the stairs a familiar smile. "Hallo, Liz. Still here, I see!"

"There's worse jobs, Mr. Barras," the girl replied, smiling back. She was a brunette in her late twenties, not especially pretty but with warmth in her face. "Nice to see you again." Her glance came to Gina, and for a brief moment registered something approaching envy before the necessities of her job took over again. "You'll find it rather warm in there tonight, miss. Would you like to leave your jacket?"

"Yes, I think I will," said Gina. She felt sorry for the girl stuck there behind that counter at this hour of the night, able only to listen to the sounds of revelry issuing from without the double swing doors some short distance away.

Ryan helped her off with the garment, the touch of his fingers against the bare skin of her shoulders like ice and fire at one the same time. She knew the other girl had seen the fleeting expression cross her face, for she smiled a little as she took the jacket and issued a ticket.

"Have a nice evening," she said.

It was difficult to gain a definite impression of the large room on the other side of the doors due to the nebulous curtain of smoke and the dim lighting. There were people dancing on a central floor and well occupied tables going back into the shadows. A waiter showed them to a table set within the curve of a padded seat against the wall, pulling it to one side to allow Gina room to slide in, then pushing it back again to imprison the two of them in their little cocoon.

"Bollinger," Ryan ordered as the waiter lifted an enquiring eyebrow.

Gina waited until the man had departed before saying lightly, "What are we celebrating?"

"The end of hostilities?" His tone was equally light.

He lifted a hand in greeting to a man just passing. "Hi there!"

The other man came to a halt at the table, glance surprised. "What are you doing in town this time of year? I expected you way back in January!"

"If I was becoming that predictable it was more than time I had a change," Ryan replied dryly. "Gina, this is Peter Moffat —Virginia Tierson."

"Hi!" This time the glance was appraising, but in a friendly fashion. "English or American?"

"Oh, English," she laughed. "Very definitely English!"

"Well, good for you. About time he left those Yankee birds alone." He gave them both a cheerful grin, apparently to rob the words of any trouble-making intent. "Playing tonight, Ryan?"

"I doubt it. We may wander through a bit later on."

"After Leila sings, you mean?" with a sage nod. "She's due on any time now. Leave you to it, then. Might see you later."

Gina stole a glance at the lean profile as the other man left, but whatever Ryan was thinking he wasn't allowing it to show. That "Yankee birds" remark might have been intended as a joke, but she didn't somehow think so. Not entirely. Yet what was it to her how many women he had known and paid attention to in his time? Their relationship was strictly of the platonic variety, his invitation tonight a means of apology and nothing else.

The arrival of the champagne created a diversion for which she was grateful at that moment, but the depression remained. She wished she had insisted on going straight home after dinner instead of allowing herself to be persuaded into coming here. Not that she had known where they were coming. Nor would it have meant anything much to her had he told her first. All she did know was that the club itself was not her environment. She felt out of her depth.

The already dimmed lighting dimmed still further as the group began playing a number recognisable to a good part of the audience, judging by the outbreak of applause. A tall, slenderly curved redhead clad in a shimmer-silver gown which fitted closely right down to her ankles stepped into the single beam of the spotlight centred just in front of the group's raised dais. She stood for a moment acknowledging the applause with a slight bow of her head before starting to sing into the hand-mike she carried.

Listening to the haunting quality of her voice, Gina found herself relaxing again, forgetting where she was and who she was with in simple enjoyment of a fine artist. There was no gimmickry, no dramatic declamation, just fine interpretation and technique. She could have listened all night.

Apparently others felt the same way, for the applause was loud and prolonged when the final song ended. But there was no encore. Leila smiled and blew a kiss, then resolutely walked off stage.

Gina turned to Ryan with praise on her lips, the latter impulse fading when she saw the faint smile lingering on his face as he watched the singer leave. Without glancing in her direction, he took out his wallet and tore a page from the notebook inside it, scribbled something on it and summoned a waiter to hand the note over.

"Give that to Leila, please," he said.

Gina forced herself to meet the grey eyes as they finally turned on her, dropping them with point to the notebook he was folding back into place.

"You never sent me that book you promised," she said, and knew her voice sounded odd. "I suppose you lost the address."

"No." He flipped back a few of the small pages and showed her the note he had made that very first night they had met, expression quizzical. "It didn't seem a good idea at the time considering the way we parted. I'd a feeling it would finish up on the rubbish heap."

"I wouldn't have done that."

"No matter how much you detested the man who'd sent it?"

"No. Anyway," she added swiftly, "I'd got over it by then."

"So you said before. Lucky you have such fleeting emotions." For a moment the lift of his lip turned him back into the man she had known those brief days seven months ago. Then he smiled and shrugged and the moment was past. "I guess it's an asset in this day and age."

"What is?" asked a husky voice. There was a silver gleam as Leila edged round on to the seat at Ryan's side without waiting to be asked to sit down. "Champagne!" she said, eyeing the bucket with lifted brows. "What's the toast?"

"Changing habits," Ryan came back imperturbably. He signalled a waiter for another glass, coming back to the striking face under its cloud of dark red hair with obvious appreciation. "You're looking great."

"More to the point, how am I sounding?" she asked on a dry note.

"Ask Gina," he said. "Her impressions are fresh."

Blue eyes looked into green with surprising steadiness. "I thought you sounded too good for this place," she said. "Why aren't you better known?"

Leila laughed suddenly. "I like her, Ryan!"

"So answer her," he said. "Why aren't you better known?"

The lovely shoulders lifted in a shrug. "Maybe I need a better agent." She lifted the glass just filled, eyeing the sparkling contents with a smile on her lips. "To success!" A moment later she added, "What happened to you in January?"

"I told you, I changed my habits. Besides, London in January isn't nearly as pleasant as this."

"It satisfied you for five years."

"Not exactly." The reply was soft. They

exchanged a look, long, intimate and filled with shared understanding, Leila was the first to break the momentary silence, looking across at Gina with an odd expression in her eyes.

"How do you cope with this guy?"

"I don't try," said Gina. Her voice felt thick in her throat. There was, or had been, something between these two; she had a feeling Ryan wished there still was. Seen in close-up, Leila was rather older than she had first thought, perhaps even around Ryan's own age, but what difference did that make with a woman of her undoubted beauty and talent? She attempted a light rejoinder. "We're just good friends."

"Now where did I hear that before?" The other voice was amused.

"Gina's going to marry a cruise ship officer," Ryan said levelly, and drew a suddenly sharpened green glance.

"Really?" Her eyes came back to Gina, expression difficult to assess. "Doesn't he mind you going out with other men while he's away? I assume he *is* away at the moment?"

Gina's shrug held a nonchalance she was far from feeling. "It isn't like that. Ryan and I aren't . . ."

"She means we aren't lovers," he cut in smoothly as she hesitated over her choice of words. "She's here tonight as a gesture of goodwill."

"I see." Whether Leila did or not remained open to speculation. She drained her glass and put it down again with a closed expression. "I'd better go and change. One more spot, then Ronald can run me home." Rising, she added to Gina, "If I don't see you again, good luck in the marriage stakes."

"She's nice," Gina ventured as the older woman moved away, and then because she couldn't stop herself, "Are she and Ronald . . ."

"They're married," Ryan said before she could finish. His tone was flat. "Have been for twelve years. He's the reason she hasn't made anything of her career, beyond this place. He preferred her with him."

Gina hesitated, sensing that she was skating on thin ice. "She must have been in agreement."

"She wouldn't let him down, if that's what you mean. Having married him she believed her career had to come second."

"That's unusal these days."

"Twelve years ago it wasn't quite as open-ended a contract. Not for Leila, at any rate. She knew the score before she married him, and was willing to settle for it. The fact that she knows she might have been a top line singer by now doesn't alter anything."

"Except to make her husband a very selfish man, perhaps."

He shrugged. "That's open to debate. I can understand his viewpoint. Why bother having a wife at all if you're hardly going to see her?"

"Surely it wouldn't have been as bad as that?"

"You don't make a career in show

business sitting at home. Anyway, she's happy enough singing here."

Was she? Gina wondered. Did this really satisfy the craving for recognition anyone with Leila's talent must feel? And where did Ryan fit into the picture? She thought she knew the answer to that one. Here was the reason he had never married himself. The way he had looked at Leila, the way he talked about her made it fairly obvious. He was in love with a woman who was already married and intended to stay that way despite her possible lapse at some time in the last five years. Leila had walked away from it; Ryan couldn't. It explained so much about him.

Why he had brought her here tonight she couldn't begin to understand. Not in the hope of proving anything to Leila, or why tell her she was going to marry another man? A whim on his part? It could only be that. Gina wished she could stop feeling so miserable.

"I think it's time I went home," she said. "It's gone midnight."

"Okay, Cinderella," he came back dryly, "I'll take you home."

Charles was missing from his desk when they left, yet Gina had the feeling that he would soon reappear should strangers attempt to enter the club. They walked up to the Strand to find a taxi, not touching this time, and not talking either. She knew his thoughts were back there in that smoke-hazed room with Leila, although he was sufficiently aware to hail a cruising taxi going in the other direction and bring it round in a sharp U-turn across the road to halt at the kerb edge.

"Please don't bother coming with me," she said quickly as he held open the door for her. "It's a long journey there and back at this time of night."

He didn't attempt to argue, simply nodded and passed in some notes to the driver before coming back to her. "Thanks for the evening," he said. There was an ironical quality to his smile. "Goodnight, Gina."

She resisted the urge to turn round and look back at him through the rear window as the taxi drew away from the kerb. Her chest felt as tight as a drum. It was over and she would probably never see him again. Even now she dared not acknowledge just how much that thought hurt.

# 8

THE weekend dragged by on leaden wings. Gina was thankful when Monday came and she could get back to work. She thought Hugh Fisher looked at her oddly when she failed to comment on the deception to which he had been a party, but he said nothing either. It was as if the whole incident had never happened. Only the knowledge that Ryan was still right here in London remained to torment her.

Mrs. Robinson had been rather short with her on Saturday morning, obviously believing her return the previous night unnecessarily late. Because it was more than likely that she would mention it to Chris in her weekly letter, Gina forestalled her by telling him about it first, omitting the fact that she had met Ryan Barras before because she had never discussed that particular episode in her life with him.

What she was going to do about Chris she wasn't at all certain. Her feelings for him could hardly be stable when another man could affect her the way Ryan had. Knowing she would not be seeing the latter again didn't help. She owed Chris wholehearted loyalty if anything at all.

The phone call came early Wednesday morning, rendering her momentarily speechless because she had not anticipated ever hearing that deep-timbred voice again.

"Gina?" Ryan asked when she failed to respond to his greeting. "That is you, isn't it?"

Her voice came back, but it sounded totally unlike her own. "Yes. Yes, it is. Did you want to speak to Hugh?"

"If I'd wanted to speak to Hugh I'd have phoned direct through to his office," he said. "I've a favour to ask."

"What?" The word came out abruptly, eliciting a slight pause on the other end of the line.

"That doesn't sound too promising," he said. "Maybe we'd better forget it."

Caution struggled with temptation and lost. Foolish or not, she couldn't bear to hear that receiver go down again at the other end without at least hearing what he had to say. "Sorry," she said. "I wasn't expecting to hear from you again. You may as well ask what you were going to ask."

"Seeing that I've already started," he finished for her on a faint note of irony. "I need somebody to type up some notes for me. Naturally, I'd expect to pay you."

It was a moment before she could bring herself to reply. "What's wrong with the agencies?"

"There's only one I ever deal with and they don't have anyone to spare right now."

"Not even for a regular customer?"

"I'm hardly that. I use them very occasionally when I happen to be in this part of the world. They're not going to pull somebody in for me at a moment's notice."

"Why a moment's notice?" she asked, playing for time. "I thought you were going to be in England for a few weeks."

"When did I say that?"

"I'm not sure. Perhaps it was just an impression I got."

"It must have been. I'm leaving for Nassau on the fifth."

Gina felt the earth fall suddenly from under her feet. "That's next week," she said hollowly.

"Six days, to be precise. I was going to leave this job till I got there, but I decided I'd rather go straight on out to the island and get started."

The island. Memory supplied a vivid mental picture of blue skies and sea, of green palms waving in the breeze. "It's little more than six months since you finished your last book," she heard herself saying.

"I told you it sometimes worked like that." The pause was brief. "Will you do it?"

He who hesitates is lost, Gina thought, and knew it was true in her case. "When?" she asked.

"Starting tonight if possible. There's a lot of it. I'll have a typewriter brought up to the suite and you can eat via room service. I'll be going out so you won't be disturbed."

She had said she would go down and spend the evening with the Robinsons tonight, Gina remembered, but that was hardly adequate reason to back out of an arrangement to which she had already half agreed. "All right, tonight," she said.

"What time do you finish—half past five?"

"I can get away at five if that's any use."

"Fine. There'll be a cab waiting for you at the main entrance. I'll still be there when you arrive, just to show you what I want. Then it's all yours." His voice had lightened. "Thanks, Gina, you've solved a problem. I didn't want to have to spend a week or so sorting out my rough notes before getting down to work. See you later."

She sat for a few minutes gazing into space after putting down the phone. She was doing herself no good at all taking on this job. It could only make things worse not better. Whatever it was that drew her and kept on drawing her to Ryan, she was going to have to get over it. In six days' time he would be gone again, this time for good so far as she was concerned. And she was going to marry Chris.

The taxi was waiting as promised on the hour. Despite the heavy traffic they reached the Hilton in under ten minutes. This time there was no need to ask at reception; she could remember the suite number as if it were imprinted in her mind. Which it probably was for all time, considering the shock she had received the first time she visited it.

Ryan opened the door to her himself, this time fully dressed in a dark blue suit with a paler shirt and a figured, self-coloured tie. Not the arty type, thank goodness. He dressed like a man, not a pseudo-tramp. She summoned a bright smile.

"Hi again!"

"Come on in," he said. His glance was distracted. "Afraid I'm going to have to get straight off—something's cropped up. My notes are over there on the desk. Hope you can read my writing. I jot the stuff down wherever I happen to be at the time the ideas come, not always with somewhere convenient to use as a rest. I want all related subject matter bringing together as far as possible. Can do?"

"Can try." If brisk impersonality was what he wanted that was what he should have. She was working for him now; obviously it made a difference. "Leave it with me."

"Good. You'll order what you want through room service, won't you. If I'm not back before you go, take a cab and charge it to me."

Back before she went? Gina reflected unemotionally as the door closed behind him. What time did he think she was going to be here till? It was five-thirty now. Eight-thirty was her limit.

She ordered sandwiches and coffee before starting work, opening the thick, loose-leafed folder to view the familiar writing with a faint smile. An aggressive hand, she imagined a calligrapher might call it: a man of strong passions and even stronger will to enforce them—yet also a man capable of admitting he was in the wrong. She wished she understood him a little better, though for what good that might do her she might as well forget it.

These were more than just notes, she realised before she had read very far. There was the whole structure of a novel contained within the hastily scrawled pages; rough, yes, but already showing some shape and form. Engrossed, she forgot the time, forgot everything but the characters she could almost see forming there before her eyes, the story slowly coming together in her mind. If this was just the bare bones what would the fiinshed article read like? She could imagine snatches of the dialogue these characters he described so vividly might speak in the circumstances in which they were to find themselves. Ryan was so good at that: his characters talked like people— real people, not cardboard cut-outs.

It was just gone eight when the phone rang. Jerked out of contemplation, Gina considered leaving it, but it seemed possible that whoever was on the other end knew there was someone in the suite, for they kept right on ringing until she had no other recourse but to lift the receiver.

"Mr. Barras's suite," she said.

There was a small pause before the unmistakable husky voice came down the line. "I want to speak to Mr. Barras. Is he there?"

"I'm afraid not. He had to go out." It was Gina's turn to pause before saying levelly, "Can I give him any message, Mrs. Conley?"

The laugh was sudden and enlightened. "Aren't you the young woman he had with him the other night? Gina, isn't it?"

"That's right." She felt impelled to add, "I'm doing some work for him."

"That's novel."

"As a matter of fact that's what I'm working on," Gina came back smartly, and heard the laugh come again.

"I'm sorry, forget the innuendo. Would you tell him I'd like to see him as soon as possible. It—it's important."

The hesitation seemed uncharacteristic,

251

but then perhaps the request in itself was unprecedented. Had Leila at last reached the end of her loyalty to her husband? Was Ryan to be the means of her escape? She was reading too much into too little, Gina tried to tell herself, and knew she was not convinced.

"I'll tell him," she said. "At least, I'll leave him the message. I won't be here when he gets back."

"He really does leave you cold, doesn't he?" said Leila. Her voice sounded odd. "That must be a new experience for Ryan. How did you two meet?"

"A long time ago and very briefly. If you ask him he'll probably tell you." Gina couldn't bring herself to be friendly. "I'm sorry, Mrs. Conley, but I have a lot to do. Would you excuse me?"

She was trembling when she put down the phone. That had been very rude, yet something in her refused to regret it. Jealousy was a soul-destroying emotion— and she was jealous, there was no getting away from it. Ryan didn't leave her cold, he never had left her cold. But he wasn't hers, and the sooner she acknowledged that he never could be the better for all concerned.

She wrote a short note to him and left it propped on the typewriter where he could hardly fail to see it, then gathered her things together and left the luxurious room without a backward glance. She wouldn't be coming back, she was determined on that. Let him find someone else to do his favours for him!

It was gone nine when she reached home. The television was turned up high in the Robinsons' flat; she could hear it through the door as she passed. It would have been a natural gesture to pop in and explain away her failure to keep the evening's arrangements—she could always say she had worked late at the office—but Mrs. Robinson was the last person she wanted to face tonight. She had to think, and think deeply, about her whole future with Chris from this point on. Once Ryan was out of her life again for good there was no doubt she would learn to forget him, only was it fair to Chris not to tell him how she felt in the hope that her feelings for him would eventually stabilise? His letters usually came on Friday or Saturday. Perhaps she should leave things till then before deciding what she was going to say to him in her reply.

She was out of the office most of the next day organising photographic sessions for a country and western group one of the larger recording companies had taken up. She got back at three to report in to Hugh Fisher with the news that everything had gone well and they were all set for a saturation attack on the pop world media.

"Good," he said absently. "A friend of yours has phoned three times while you've been out. Going to phone him back?"

"If you mean Ryan Barras, the answer is no," Gina stated firmly, and drew a speculative glance.

"Your business, I suppose. Only I don't think he's going to give up that easily."

Gina hesitated in the doorway, back half turned. "Do you know him very well, Hugh?"

"I don't see him often enough for that.

We've had a few drinks together, and I've taken him home to dinner once or twice. Sheila and the girls think he's the cat's whiskers."

"Along with half the female population of the world, by all accounts."

The chuckle was rich. "If you believe all you hear after working here for a year or more you're more gullible than I thought. A man doesn't get to be thirty-four and unmarried without sowing a few wild oats, but he'd need to be Superman to keep up with his press coverage!" He lifted a pair of quizzical eyebrows at her as the phone rang. "This is probably him again. He said he'd ring after three. Want to speak to him?"

Gina shook her head, aware she was being ridiculous yet unable to make the effort to stop it. "No."

Nevertheless she stayed there hovering in the doorway as Hugh picked up the receiver, watching his face.

"She's back," he said, "but she doesn't want to speak to you." He listened a moment, face wearing an infuriatingly

255

bland expression, then said, "You could be right." Replacing the receiver, he looked across at her with the same expression. "Still here?"

"What did he say?" The question was torn from her. Hugh shrugged. "He said women are the devil."

"Was that all?"

"What else did you expect? Opposition doesn't always elicit renewed effort. Sometimes it has the opposite effect."

"It isn't like that," she said, and knew he did not believe her.

She stayed until close on six making up for lost time on the back-log of work on her desk. Hugh was still there when she left. He waved a hand in farewell as she passed the glass partition.

Despite the passing traffic, the evening air was balmy, the sky overhead a clear pale blue scarcely shadowed as yet by approaching night. Gina felt like making for open space; somewhere quiet where she could breathe. Anywhere but the solitude of her flat with only the prospect of Mrs. Robinson's approaching footsteps to look forward to.

The hand which came under her elbow from behind was hard and purposeful. Without turning round she knew at once who it was.

"You owe me an explanation," Ryan said close by her ear. He sounded distinctly grim. "I've been waiting here for the last damned hour!"

"I had some work to complete," Gina said stiffly. "How was I to know?"

"That wasn't the explanation I was talking about. There's a little matter of a note you left me last night."

She turned her head then, to meet chilly grey eyes. "So I changed my mind. You'll find someone else."

"Not in time. And you said you'd take the job on."

"I said I'd come last night, that was all."

"Don't split hairs," on a note of impatience. "You agreed, and you're darned well going to finish it!"

"Why don't you do it yourself?" she

257

suggested. "You can type, because I've seen you, and you'd know far better than anyone else how to correlate your material." Her voice hardened. "Or do you have other things to do?"

He looked at her for a long moment, expression assessing. "We can't discuss anything here in the street," he said at length. "I'll get a cab."

"You'll be lucky, this time of day." She waved a hand in the direction of the thronging traffic. "See any flags up?"

"All right," he said, "from Brompton Road to Park Lane isn't that far. If necessary we'll walk."

"I have to get home," she protested, and recognised the futility even as she said it. "Ryan, I don't *want* to do this job for you!"

"Why? No"—he held up a staying hand —"we'll talk about it later. Come on."

Perhaps fortunately they managed to get a taxi on the corner of Hans Road, getting in ahead of three other would-be customers who wasted time in asking the driver how long it would take to get to St.

Pancras. To compensate for the shorter trip—or perhaps because it was habitual to him—Ryan gave the man an excellent tip when they reached the hotel.

The suite's sitting room looked exactly as she had left it the previous evening, the typewriter sitting squarely in the centre of the desk Ryan had had brought in, the loose-leaf folder closed beside it.

"Take off your coat," he invited on a note which indicated he might do it for her if she didn't comply. "Are you hungry?"

"Not yet." She slipped off the pale green coat which matched her skirt and slung it over a chair arm, standing there a little defiantly, hair just brushing the collar of her silky cream blouse. "I'm not thirsty either."

"I didn't offer you a drink."

"You mean the hired help doesn't rate alcohol?"

A faint sardonic smile touched his lips. "I could always send down for some wine. How about a nice dry white?"

"Louse," she said bitterly. "I wondered

259

how long it would take you to revert to type!"

"And now you've found out—so far as you're aware." He studied her, expression disquieting. "Why, Gina? Why the change of mind? You seemed willing enough yesterday, and I know you went through my notes because some of the sheets had been clipped together. Did it bore you so much?"

"No, of course it didn't bore me." The denial was instructive, almost indignant.

"Then it had to be something else." He paused. "Leila's phone call, perhaps? She said you sounded short."

"I was busy, that's all. I didn't have time to chat. I passed the message on, what more did she want?"

"Odd," he said. "I got the impression you rather liked her the other night."

"I admire her talent—and her looks. I imagine most people do."

"Generally speaking, other females aren't always so generous. She has been known to arouse quite a bit of the old green-eye."

"The moral of which is don't let future girl-friends see you drooling over her." Gina didn't much care what she said; she wanted to hurt. "Always providing there'll be others now."

Enlightenment dawned suddenly in the grey eyes. "So that's it! You thought she was going to ask me to take her away from Ronald. And it mattered to you."

"Not that way," she denied fiercely, and realised she had been too vehement when she saw the slow smile widen his mouth. She put up her hands to fend him off as he advanced on her, backing away until her knees came into sharp contact with the edge of the chesterfield. "No, Ryan. Leave me alone!"

"No way," he said. "I thought I was going to have to spend all week working up to this through all those layers of protection you've built round you."

He pulled her resistingly towards him, finding her mouth with unerring aim, arms unyielding to her attempts to free herself. After a moment she no longer wanted to free herself. She kissed him back hungrily, body pressing closer, unable to have enough of him. Regrets could come later. This was now and she wanted him. She had always wanted him. She always would want him.

When he lifted her on to the chesterfield she made no protest, looking up into the lean face above her with a sense of time standing still, feeling the touch of his hands warm against her skin, long sensitive fingers sliding gently around her back to unhook the single catch. The grey eyes were filled with tiny dancing lights, his mouth curved to a line which made her reach up and draw him down to her, her own eyes wincing at the touch that was almost agony.

She opened her mouth to whisper his name, and felt her whole body suddenly stiffen as memory swept over her. It was happening again, just like before. In another minute he would lift his head and look at her with that same withering scorn as she lay there defenceless under his gaze. Only this time she was ahead of him.

She took him totally by surprise as she

pushed him strongly away and sat up, so much so that she had herself covered before he reacted.

"Why?" he asked on a rough note.

"Because I owe you that," she said, equally roughly. "Hell, isn't it?"

His whole face hardened to a sudden frightening mask, a muscle jerking close by his mouth. "You damned little vixen," he muttered. "You did that on purpose!"

"Strange, isn't it, that the feminine sounds so much more vicious than the masculine? Now you know what it feels like."

"No," he said, "not yet. But I intend to."

"I don't think so. Not in a Hilton suite. You have your name to think of. Affairs are one thing, rape quite another. Ask Hugh—he'll tell you the same."

"I don't need to ask Hugh anything. I wasn't talking about rape."

"Oh, of course, you never found the need to use force on a woman, did you?" Considering the fact that she was unable to swing her feet to the ground while he still sat there she was in no position to be taunting him, but something drove her on regardless. "I think I just proved nothing less is going to work with me."

"You proved nothing—unless it's your sheer, mule-headed obstinacy." The anger had faded a little, but there was enough of a threat left in his eyes to make her bite what she had been about to say next. "That wasn't all pretence a moment ago. Your body was saying yes even if your mind had other plans. It would be interesting to see which was stronger in the long run—will or want. What would it take, I wonder, to get you to the point of no return?"

"I don't know." The driving desire to hurt had drained from her as suddenly and swiftly as if someone had pulled a plug, leaving her sick with disgust at her own actions. "Not a lot, apparently, when it comes down to it. Let me go, Ryan. I want to go home."

"Are you sure?" His voice was level again, expression difficult to qualify. "Can this sailor of yours really satisfy you?"

"I don't know," she said again. "We haven't gone that far. Anyway, there's more to marriage than sex."

"Tell me the other essential ingredients."

"Compatibility for one."

Ryan said dryly, "When two people agree on everything one of them is superfluous."

"That wasn't what I meant. People can agree to disagree, can't they?"

"Some might. I doubt if you're one of them." He had an arm stretched across her to the back of the chesterfield, effectively blocking her escape. "What else?"

She met his gaze unflinchingly. "Security."

Something flickered in the grey eyes. "Maybe you should have put that first. It obviously means a lot to you."

"No more than it should. Everyone likes to feel safe."

"Even if it's dull?" He waited a moment, watching her face, before going on softly, "You know, the one thing you haven't mentioned is the only one that's

265

supposed to be important to a woman. I take it you're not in love with this Chris?"

Her face burned suddenly. "Of course I'm in love with him. I took it for granted it didn't have to be said."

"You're a liar." His tone was flat, denying contradiction. "You found a man you thought could give you an adequate life-style, and in the absence of anything better you settled for him. Either some part of your friend Marie's attitude rubbed off on you, or you already had it right there in you, but if you go ahead and marry this guy you're not all that much better than she was!"

He was right and she knew it. She couldn't marry Chris because she didn't love him, and without love the rest wasn't enough. Knowing it and admitting it, however, were two very different things. She made her voice deliberately light and uncaring.

"So what would you suggest I did instead?"

He said it so calmly she could scarcely

believe she had heard him correctly at first. "You can come with me next week."

How long she sat there staring at him, Gina could not afterwards have said. It seemed like whole minutes but was probably only seconds.

"That's not much of a joke," she managed at last.

He smiled faintly. "I'm not joking. The offer's open. Of course, it doesn't include security, and it almost certainly wouldn't include total compatibility, but we have enough going for us to make it worthwhile. You already know my requirements. What was it you called it? A mouse by day a wife by night—in a manner of speaking."

Gina still couldn't believe he was serious. Things like this didn't happen to people like her. But they did, she recalled. Seven months ago far less realistic things had happened to her. What Ryan was suggesting was in no way fantastic set against that previous experience. It probably wasn't even the first time.

"The word is mistress," he said, assessing the point her thoughts had reached with some accuracy. "A bit old-fashioned these days, but still the most accurate way to describe the relationship. Unless you'd prefer 'living in sin'?"

"Stop it!" The anger was swift and all-consuming, the hurt a barbed hook deep inside her. "You must be mad if you really think I'd sink to that!"

"There'd be no sinking about it. We'd both be getting the same out of it. The weekends we'd spend in Nassau doing all the things you ever craved to do, weekdays you could swim and sunbathe and just generally laze around while I work. And at night"—he paused and smiled—"well, that's best left to spontaneity."

There was some quality about that smile of his she didn't fully comprehend. Not humour, for certain. "This wasn't a spontaneous idea, was it?" she asked with bitterness. "You knew just what you were going to say!"

"True. I came here to find you again. Admittedly you threw me a little when you announced you were getting married, but

I soon realised the decision wasn't exactly irreversible."

"Why me?" she demanded hollowly. "There must be dozens who'd jump at the chance."

"If there are, they're not the ones I want. I just spent seven months trying to forget a little blonde castaway, without success. This is the only way I'm going to get her out of my system."

"No, it isn't, because I don't accept."

"You're going to marry Chris instead?"

"Whatever I do, you won't be here to see it. Now will you please move and let me get up?"

"Not without adding a little weight to my side of the question."

She fought him as he pressed her down into the cushions again, but he was too big and too strong to resist for long. By the time he'd finished with her she had no defences left, except one. "I hate you," she whispered fiercely, and saw him smile.

"I know. But you want me just as badly as I want you, and that's all I'm interested in proving at the moment. Not here like this. I can get casual sex any time. I want you there on the island with me, Gina."

"For how long?" her question came despite herself.

"For as along as it takes."

She knew what he meant. Who could set a limit on that kind of relationship? It might last a week, it might last a month, it might even last longer than that. But eventually it would end because there was nothing else to hold it together.

"The answer is still no," she said.

"Think about it. You've got till Tuesday." He stood up then, tall, lean and arrogant, and so totally in command of the situation. "I'll phone down for a cab."

"What about the work you wanted me to do?" Gina asked, coming to her feet unsteadily.

"You mean you'd still consider it?" He shook his head, irony in the line of his mouth. "Forget it. It was just a ruse to get you here in the first place. I work direct from rough notes."

"I ought to have burned them," she said bitterly.

"If you had I'd probably be in custody charged with murder right now," he came back. "Feel flattered I even let you near them under the circumstances. If I hadn't known you had feeling for the written word I might have felt bound to find some other means of enticing you."

He dialled a number, spoke briskly into the phone, then replaced the receiver and glanced back at her. "There'll be a cab waiting for you when you get down. I take it you won't want me to come down with you?"

"No." Gina finished fastening her coat and picked up her handbag from the chair. She made herself look at him. "Goodbye, Ryan."

"I'll be in touch."

"The answer will still be the same."

He shrugged lightly. "That's a bridge I'll have to cross when I come to it."

She didn't bother arguing any further. What was the use? He could bring her close to surrender here in this room, but once she was away from him there was no chance. It might have been different had she been in love with him, but she wasn't. How could she love a man who would do this to her?

# 9

SHE was to ask herself that question many times over the following days still without finding an adequate answer. Chris's letter arriving on Saturday morning provided no help.

He was full of the cruise, obviously enjoying every minute of his new job. From Piraeus they were to sail to Messina on the island of Sicily, then across to Naples where the passengers would disembark for the flight home. The ship would be there now, Gina realised, waiting for another load of passengers to embark, this time to sail a slightly different route. She would not be seeing Southampton again until the end of the season, although Chris himself would be flown home on leave in July. Three months on and one off was the rule. From the way he spoke three months would pass both swiftly and pleasantly for him.

Gina made one decision that weekend. Waiting three months until Chris came home to tell him what she had to tell him was fair on neither of them. She was going to have to look for somewhere else to live, of course; it would hardly be possible to stay on here under the circumstances.

Ryan's proffered alternative she resolutely put to the back of her mind. Even if he had been serious, and that was still open to doubt, she had no intention of letting herself in for the inevitable misery which would be hers when he eventually tired of her. Men like Ryan didn't form lasting relationships. They needed to keep their options open. Let him find someone else to provide solace for his lonely hours!

The letter to Chris took a lot of composing. Achieving honesty while trying not to hurt any further than was absolutely necessary took a lot of doing. She wasn't at all satisfied with the finished result but it would have to do. Perhaps she should have got Ryan to write it for her, she reflected ironically. He'd no doubt have known exactly how to put it.

The latter rang her at the office on Monday afternoon when she had just about managed to convince herself that the whole thing had been a sick joke on his part.

"I told you I'd be in touch," he said. "Don't give me your answer now. Come and have dinner with me tonight and tell me then."

"Tonight or now, it's going to be the same," she said, steeling herself against the ache his voice alone elicited. "I don't want to see you again, Ryan."

"Because you're scared you might weaken?"

"If you like." There was little point in denying it. "Your offer is too one-sided."

"So you're going to marry Chris after all?"

"Yes." As a face-saver that statement left a lot to be desired, but it was all she had. "Aren't you going to wish me luck?"

"What I wish you is neither here nor there at the moment." He paused. "If you change your mind there'll be a ticket waiting for you at that travel agency a couple of blocks from the office for a month from tomorrow. All you'll have to do is give them your name, and they'll book you a flight."

She said thickly, "You just can't take no for an answer, can you?"

"Apparently not." The pause was brief, his voice when it came on again suddenly cynical. "Seems like I might have been backing a wrong hunch. Goodbye, Gina."

The click of the replaced receiver had a finality about it which numbed her. She tried to tell herself she was glad it was all over and she knew she lied. She wanted desperately to be on that plane with him tomorrow, only she didn't have the courage to take that kind of chance. That was what it all boiled down to.

She went through the rest of the week without thinking of anything much at all beyond the immediate demands of her job. It was difficult to avoid contact with the Robinsons, but she managed it somehow by staying in town in the evenings and pretending to be in too much of a hurry to talk on the one morning Mrs. Robinson did waylay her. They would have to know eventually, of course, but until she heard from Chris it would hardly be fair to say anything, and she couldn't bring herself to pretend that everything was all right.

Friday morning brought a totally unexpected phone call from Leila Conley.

"I'd like to see you," the singer announced. "Can we meet somewhere after you finish work?"

"To talk about what?" Gina asked coolly.

"Ryan. I believe you're labouring under a misapprehension regarding my relationship with him."

"If I am it isn't really important any longer," Gina came back. "He's gone."

"But I haven't, and it's important to me." The husky voice paused. "Make it Speakers' Corner at six. We can walk down to Victoria Gate and talk on the way. I must go now, I'm supposed to be rehearsing."

Gina spent the day in a state of flux, one minute deciding to keep the appointment, the next asking herself what difference it would make. She was still undecided when she emerged from the office at five-forty, and only the unusual sight of a taxi coming around the corner open for business finally made up her mind.

Leila was there before her, the red hair tucked up under a close-fitting cloche-type hat which matched her twenties-style suit. In daylight it was possible to see the tiny lines beginning to radiate from the corners of her eyes, although her make-up was impeccable. She was older than Ryan, Gina realised—perhaps by as much as five or six years. Not that that meant anything. Lots of men were attracted to older women.

"Let's walk," Leila said.

Moving at her side along the Ring, Gina waited until the only other stroller in sight had passed them before saying levelly, "What was it you wanted to tell me?"

"I was just wondering how to begin," Leila confessed with a wry smile. "I suppose to start with I wanted to tell you that Ryan and I don't have any kind of affair going. When I rang him the other night it was because I needed his advice, nothing else. You see, after all these years I was actually considering leaving Ronald and trying to make something of a career outside the club. Kind of now-or-never panic, I suppose you could call it. When a woman hits forty she starts to feel that way about life in general—starts thinking of all the things she might have done and didn't." Her glance held a mild envy. "At your age you've got it all in front of you. Don't waste it."

There was little Gina could say. She believed her because it rang so true. At least regarding now it did. Some time in the past she still suspected there had been a little more than simple friendship between Leila and Ryan, but that was something she would probably never know for sure.

"What did Ryan advise?" she asked at length.

Leila laughed. "He was typically blunt about it. Said I'd left it too late and to stick to what I had."

"Too late?" For a moment Gina was

almost indignant. "But your voice is great! And you don't look anywhere near forty."

"Thanks." The tone was just a little dry. "He meant it was too late to start building a whole career. You're in promotions; you should know what he was getting at. Ten years ago I might have managed it, not now. I have a name of sorts and I'm going to be satisfied with that."

Gina said softly, "You must have loved your husband very much."

"Yes, I did—and still do, now the panic is over. There have been times in the past when I've wished I'd never met him, and I daresay there'll be plenty more in the future, but essentially we have a good marriage." She paused, glancing sideways. "Does any of this help you?"

"No," Gina admitted. "Not a lot. Did Ryan ask you to speak to me?"

"No, it was my own idea. He told me he'd asked you to marry him and you'd turned him down."

"Marry?" It was Gina's turn to laugh. "Either he was lying his head off or you misunderstood what he said. He asked me to go with him. Marriage certainly wasn't mentioned."

"Oh." Leila seemed to consider, an odd expression on her face. Finally she said, "Is it too late to take him up on the offer?"

"No, I have a month to make up my mind. He even left me a plane ticket with an agency in case I changed it."

"But you're not going to?"

"No." Gina hesitated, glancing at the older woman uncertainly. "Would you?"

"I don't know. He must want you with him very badly."

"Want is the operative word!"

"Well, it's a start. Great oaks from little acorns grow." Leila was smiling faintly. "It's for certain you're not going to make him fall in love with you over thousands of miles."

"It's not certain I could do it anyway."

"That's a chance you'd have to take— always providing you were in love with him in the first place." Leila held up a staying hand. "I'm not asking—that's your own business. It's all your own business. All I wanted to do was make sure my part in it wasn't misunderstood. Have I succeeded?"

"Yes."

"That's good. The rest is up to you." Leila glanced at her watch. "I'm going to have to fly."

"You carry on, then," Gina suggested. "I'll walk down slowly." She added softly, "And thanks for making the effort, even if you did mistake his motives."

"That's all right. I owe Ryan a lot one way or another." Leila smiled and lifted a hand. "Remember what I said—don't waste it!"

That could be taken two ways, Gina reflected as the other woman moved swiftly on ahead. She could waste months of her life on Ryan only to finish up on her own again when he decided he wanted out. Yet mightn't it almost be worth it? a treacherous little voice asked. Better a few months of paradise than none at all.

She was home by seven, unable to face the idea of another evening passing time in town. Mrs. Robinson must have heard her come in, but her door remained firmly closed. Gina couldn't blame her. Her own behaviour this last couple of weeks had been distinctly unsociable.

There was a letter from Chris in her box. She took off her coat and made herself some coffee before opening it.

After she had read it for the second time she sat for several moments trying to work out how she felt. Shock, yes, she finally decided, but no pain. In fact relief might be the closest word to describe her reaction. In essence Chris had said the same things she had said a week ago in her letter to him. The crazy thing was that they had both been posted on the same day. Two minds thinking alike yet thousands of miles apart. Telepathy must have been at work. Without it the coincidence was just too great.

"*Don't think too badly of me*, Chris had written. *I was the one who made all the running and now I'm the one who wants to pull out. It isn't that I don't still think a whole lot of you, Gina. You'll always be special. What I do need is a few more years of freedom before I finally settle down. I hope you'll understand.*

Oh yes, she understood. More than he would ever know. He wanted to sow his wild oats while he had the chance, with no thoughts of a wife waiting trustingly at home to prick his conscience. Well, why not? At least he was being honest with himself—and with her.

He would probably have her letter by now. She had sent it to reach him when they docked in Tripoli, and that had been today. She wondered what his feelings were at present. Not that it mattered any longer. They were both of them free as air, free to do anything they wanted.

There was a tentative knock on the door and Mrs. Robinson popped her head round, her pleasant, homely features wearing an uncomfortable expression.

"Can I come in?" she asked.

"Yes, of course." Gina got up from the chair. "I've just made some coffee. Would you like some?"

"Please." Her eyes were fixed on the pages Gina had laid down on the arm before she rose. "I don't know what to say about that boy of mine. He ought to be shot, doing a thing like this!"

So he'd informed his mother of his intentions too. Gina thought. All square and above board. She squashed down the fleeting reflection that he might have waited. Perhaps he'd believed she might need comforting, though his mother was hardly the person to put in that particular position.

"You know you don't mean that," she said. "Chris hasn't done anything wrong. Anyone is entitled to change their mind."

Uncertainty crossed the other face. "I must say, you don't seem all that upset."

"Perhaps because Chris's letter took a load off my mind," Gina admitted. She brought the mug of coffee across to where Mrs. Robinson had perched uncomfortably on the edge of the other chair, looking down into the puzzled eyes. "You see, we'd both decided we made a mistake. I wrote to Chris telling him so the same day he posted this."

It was a moment or two before any

answer came. Conflicting emotions showed clearly on her face. Relief was there, true, but mingled with it was more than a hint of indignation. Gina hid a faint smile. For Chris to break things off was bad, but for her to reject the son she adored, that was bordering on insult.

"Well, you're a real pair," came the comment at last. "Still, I suppose it was better you found out now than after you were married."

"Infinitely better," Gina agreed. She hesitated before adding, "You'll understand why I felt it would be a good thing if I looked for somewhere else to live, though, don't you? No matter how much we were in agreement, we'd be bound to feel a bit strange with one another living in the same house, more or less."

"He won't be home most of the year," his mother pointed out. "They're doing the South American cruise over Christmas, and the Canaries after that."

"I know. I just feel it would be better."

"Well, it's up to you." Mrs. Robinson

paused, added sadly, "I'll miss you, but you know best what you want."

Did she? Gina wondered. Right now she wasn't at all sure.

Alone again, she tried to keep her thoughts from turning to Ryan, but it proved impossible. Eventually she discarded all attempts and let her mind roam free, remembering the days they had spent together on the island, the breathtaking beauty of the lagoon, the shabby comfort of the little house.

And then, because she couldn't stop herself, she thought of how it felt to have his arms about her, his lips on hers, his hands on her body; possessive; conjuring emotions she had never felt in depth before. She remembered his voice, not just in passion but in conversation, the way his eyes took on that wonderful intensity when he spoke of his work, the way his hair fell across his forehead in that thick dark comma which made her want to reach out a hand and brush it back. He could be so many different people, and she loved them all. Yes *loved*. If she hadn't admitted it before it was only because she didn't dare.

Don't waste it, Leila had said. Take a chance. *Dared* she?

It was three o'clock in the morning before she finally reached a conclusive decision. Leila was right, wanting was a start. She could make Ryan love her if she worked at it. She had to make him love her. And if he didn't—well she would cross that bridge when she came to it.

He was waiting for her at the airport when she landed a fortnight later. Seeing him standing there in the long, low entrance hall, she felt almost like turning and running back on to the plane again. His smile only half dispelled the strangeness. He looked different somehow; he even acted different. Or was it just her own uncertainty that made it appear so?

"Neil sends his regards," he said as he drove the Lotus Elan away from the car park. "He's away on business at the moment, but he's given me free loan of his house for the next few days, plus his staff. I thought you might appreciate a little high living here in Nassau before we go out to the island."

"You haven't started your book yet?" Gina asked.

"No." His mouth twisted. "Somehow I couldn't get down to it—guess I had other things on my mind." He glanced at her briefly. "Your letter didn't say a great deal. How did Hugh take it?"

"In his stride."

"You told him you were coming out here?"

"I didn't have to. He seemed to know already."

"Not from me."

Gina could believe that. Ryan wasn't the type to go round bragging his conquests, especially by mail. She said, "He let me off with a fortnight's notice anyway."

"Good of him."

"Wasn't it?" The conversation was so stilted it was becoming ridiculous, Gina thought on an edge of desperation. Why had she come? She barely knew this man. She stole a glance at the hard-cut profile, moving down to the hands lightly grasping the wheel. She had put her life in those hands. What kind of fool was she? "It's a nice car," she said. "Yours?"

"Hired."

She stopped trying after that, looking out of the window at the skeleton finger of a windmill pump sticking out above the pines and recalling her initial disappointment on first seeing this bare central part of New Providence on the way from the airport all those months ago. Little had she known then what was in store for her. She wondered how Marie was doing. Probably she was better off not knowing. Wherever she was, Marie would not have lost out.

Neil's house lay a short distance along the coast east of Nassau, possessing no sea frontage but making up for the lack with a large, oval-shaped pool in an exceedingly lovely garden. The house itself was colonial style, with white pillars supporting a south-facing balcony on to which all the bedrooms this side of the house opened. From it the sea looked turquoise, sparkling under the rays of the afternoon sun.

"Like it?" asked Ryan from the doorway behind her. "It's beautiful," she said without turning round. "Neil must feel lost, just him and three servants."

"Not for much longer. He's selling the place. He met a widow in Miami and she doesn't want to leave the mainland."

"Perhaps she'd change her mind if she saw this place."

"I doubt it. Apparently her own house is half as big again, and with a private beach."

"Lucky Neil!"

"I haven't met the woman, so I can't say whether he is or not. He seems happy enough with the arrangement." Ryan paused, and she heard him move, felt his hands on her shoulders turning her back to him. The grey eyes held a strange expression. "Something I should have done at the airport," he said, "but you looked anything but ready."

Gina closed her eyes as he drew her to

him. The kiss reassured her. Whatever the future held, he wanted her now.

"I thought you'd changed your mind," she murmured when he let her go again. "You seemed so indifferent."

"Calculating I might be," he came back, "fickle I'm not."

Gina wished she could believe that. He probably believed it himself right now. "What happened to Pal?" she asked suddenly, remembering. "You didn't leave him alone on the island, did you?"

"Hardly. I put him in kennels for a few days. We'll collect him when we leave. How about a swim? You'll have plenty of time to dry your hair before we go out tonight." He smiled a little at her suddenly wary expression. "No, on our own. It's time you sampled the real Nassau."

And afterwards they would drive back here to this lovely house and share the king-sized bed in there. Gina wished they could have gone straight out to the island. It would be different there, she was sure of it.

Ryan changed while she busied herself

searching for a bikini in one of her suitcases, tossing a thick terry robe on to the bed from the bathroom door and slinging another over a shoulder.

"I'll see you down there. Bring that with you. They're better than any towel."

The bikini was new, dull yellow in colour and very brief. She regretted her lack of a proper tan to complement it, although some of last year's colour still lingered. Anyway she wouldn't be long in acquiring one now she was here. What was it Ryan had said? Nothing to do all day but swim and sunbathe and generally laze around. He wouldn't want her clattering about the house while he worked, that was for sure. Only at night would she be called upon to perform any duties, and she could hardly pretend she would find them exactly distasteful.

Ryan was in the pool when she got down. He hoisted himself on to the side and watched her coming, water dripping from the slicked-back hair on to bronzed shoulders.

"I've ordered tea and sandwiches

293

brought out in fifteen minutes or so," he said. "Nothing like a bathe to work up an appetite."

Selfconscious under his gaze, Gina dropped her robe and kicked off her sandals, poised for a brief moment on the edge, then executed a neat shallow dive into water totally lacking in the kind of cold one might automatically anticipate in England. When she surfaced, Ryan had gone from his perch.

Even as she twisted in the water to look for him he came up right beside her. With his six inches of superior height he could stand on the bottom at this particular spot, giving him an unfair advantage as he reached for her. Gentle at first, his kiss slowly deepened until response became pure blind instinct on her part. She scarcely felt the touch of his fingers at her back, only the silky swirl of the water over her bare skin as her bikini top came free.

"The servants," she gasped, trying to pull away. "Ryan . . ." He drew the thin straps down over her arms and tossed the garment lightly on to the side, bringing her back against him and watching her eyes dilate with a narrowed intensity in his own. "Damn the servants," he muttered thickly. "Why didn't you come sooner?"

"I couldn't." Her senses were doing the swimming right now, every one of the thickly curling hairs on his chest a separate instrument of torment. "Ryan, please . . ." He hoisted her higher in the water to kiss each hardened nipple before letting her go. "You'll get used to it," he said.

She kept her back to him as she climbed out and reached for the robe, belting it around her numbly. She could hardly complain. She had given Ryan carte blanche to act that way by coming here to him like this in the first place. He hadn't lied, he hadn't pretended anything. He had laid it right on the line. So far as he was concerned her body was his to do as he liked with for as long as they stayed together.

He stayed in the pool swimming lazily up and down the length while she sat on one of the sumptuously padded loungers and watched him, almost hating him for the power he had to stir her. Back in London she had been so sure love was enough to get her through. Here nothing was the same. But it was too late now to start changing her mind. She had no means of getting home again.

The tea and sandwiches arrived. Borne by a middle-aged Nassauvian answering to the name of Joseph. He was polite but withdrawn. Censure? Gina wondered. The servants would know they weren't married. What did they think of her?

Ryan came to join her, using the sleeve of his robe to rub his hair before slinging it about his shoulders.

"This is one English habit I'll not decry," he said, tasting the fragrant brew. "Joe really does it well."

"I think he disapproves of us," Gina observed huskily, and felt his glance on her.

"Does that bother you?"

"A little."

There was a brief silence before he said on a suddenly harder note, "Maybe we should have gone straight out to the island after all. Too late tonight."

"We could go tomorrow."

"Is that what you want?"

She didn't look at him. "Yes."

"Then we'll go tomorrow." He drained his cup and replaced it in the saucer with a decisive clink. "You ought to go and rest after that flight. We shan't be going out before eight-thirty. Wear that silvery thing you had on the night we went to the club, will you? It looked good on you."

"All right." For a moment she contemplated telling him that Leila had contacted her, then decided against it. It had no bearing on the present position. She got to her feet. "I think you're right about that rest. I do feel a bit tired."

"I won't disturb you," he said. "Just sling my things out on the chest beside the door and I'll use one of the other bedrooms. I'll be up about eight to change."

Only when she reached the bedroom did she realise she had left her bikini top draped casually over the arm of the lounger she had used. What Joseph would make of that she hated to think. Unless Ryan had the sense to bring it up with him when he came to get his things. Not that he probably cared a jot for what Joseph might think.

She had a shower and washed her hair, towelling it almost dry before brushing it into smooth order. Her eyes in the mirror looked bruised. Not unexpected after the long flight from England perhaps, but could that also account for the pit of depression into which her spirits had sunk? Perhaps things would look brighter again after a nap. She could only hope so.

It was dark when she awoke, the soft darkness she remembered so well. Familiar sounds and scents filtered in through the window screens. The luminous fingers of her watch said it was a quarter past seven. She felt refreshed for the sleep but no happier. The same problems existed.

She was all ready in the silver-grey dress when Ryan came up to change. He made no protests when she said she would wait for him downstairs, but his mouth took on the sardonic slant she so disliked.

Downstairs she wandered through the several luxurious rooms with a sense of trespass because Neil wasn't here to make it right. The sitting room was enormous, with sliding glass doors giving on to a wide flagged terrace which in turn overlooked the garden and pool. Joseph came into the room while she was looking out, impassive features revealing no flicker of surprise on finding her there.

Gina shook her head when he asked if she would like a drink, then on impulse asked, "Have you been with Mr. Davids long, Joseph?"

"Since he first came to this house, mam. That's fifteen years now."

"Shall you stay on with the new owners, do you think?"

"That depends on who buys the place, mam." His voice was quiet, with only a slight blurring of the consonants to distinguish it from an Englishman's. His expression never altered a fraction. "Will there be anything else, mam?"

Gina shook her head again, recognising that she was not going to get through to the man in any way. Her presence here under these conditions was an affront he accepted only because he had been ordered to do so. There was no doubting that she would not be the only one to feel relief when they left.

Ryan was wearing the combination of dark trousers and white dinner jacket she found so devastating when he came down. Looking at him she felt her heart turn over. If only things could have been different, if they could have met and fallen in love in the normal way, this might even have been their honeymoon instead of the start of a sordid affair. Yes, sordid. There was nothing beautiful about their relationship. She knew then what she was going to do—what she had to do to save her own self-respect.

Ryan didn't speak much on the way into town—perhaps because she had little to say herself. They went to one of the grandest of the big hotels, not quite so packed out with millionaires as it would have been a month or two ago but still redolent enough of wealth.

The meal Ryan chose was no doubt delicious, certainly wildly expensive, but so far as Gina was concerned totally wasted as she barely tasted a thing. She refused all but one glass of wine, knowing she must keep a clear head for what was to come. It wasn't going to be easy to say what she had to say, but there was no other way.

"You're not enjoying this one bit, are you?" Ryan asked when they danced after they'd finished coffee. "Do you want to go?"

"Yes," she said. "But not back to the house. At least, not straight away. I—I have to talk to you. Ryan."

He looked down at her for a long moment, expression undergoing an indefinable change. "About what?"

"Not here. Please."

"All right."

He led her off the floor back to their table and called over the waiter. Bare minutes later they were in the car and heading along the coast towards Delaport Point. The ripple-edged tarmac gave a hard ride even in a car like this one. Eventually Ryan found a sandy track leading off into the casuarinas and parked on the edge of a beach, switching off the engine before turning to her.

"Okay," he said, "let's have it."

Gina drew in a steadying breath. His gaze was unnerving. "I want to go back home," she said at last, and was surprised that the words came out calmly. "I realise it's asking a lot considering that it's already cost you the price of my ticket out here, but I'll pay you back given time."

"Why?" His voice was unexpectedly gentle. "What changed your mind, Gina?"

She looked at him then for the first time, throat contracting as she met the grey eyes. It had to be the truth; nothing else would do. She knew already what his reaction would be. He would smile and shrug, perhaps a little wryly, she hoped not mockingly, and then he would tell her whether or not she was free to go. If he refused regardless she wasn't sure what she was going to do.

"I just can't go through with it," she said. Her laugh sounded raw. "It's ironical when you think about it. I couldn't marry Chris because I didn't love him, and I can't stay here with you because I do."

She had faced front again before she spoke, gaze fixed on the silver-streaked sea beyond the half moon of white beach. The silence seemed to last a long time. When Ryan's hand came out and took her chin to turn her face towards him she put up no resistance. In the shadowed light his face was hard to read.

"Why should loving me make any difference?"

"Because for you it's just physical, and I can't take it. I thought I could, but . . . I can't, that's all. This afternoon in the pool—the way Joseph looks at me . . . I feel like a whore!"

"They don't have feelings," he said. "They do it for the money. When did you decide it was love you felt for me?"

"Before I wrote to tell you I was coming, or I wouldn't have come."

"And now you want to go again for the same reason."

"Yes."

Impossible to make him understand. She doubted if he believed a word she had said. "I know I've cost you a lot of money and given nothing in return, but I . . ."

"To hell with the money!" He said it harshly, but the anger did not seem directed at her. He let her go, sitting back in his seat with a raw laugh of his own. "I asked for that, bringing you out here this way. It was one hell of a lousy stunt to pull."

"Stunt?" She was bewildered.

"That's right." He paused. "If I'd asked you to marry me the last time we were together would you have accepted?"

She sat very still, unable to take in what he seemed to be implying. "I don't know," she said at last.

"I didn't dare risk it. If you'd said yes I'd never have known for certain whether you simply considered me a better bargain than Chris."

"You couldn't have believed that," she protested. "Not after the way I was with you that night."

His smile was faint. "I was taking that into account as part of the bargain. I knew I could stir you sexually, I just had to be sure it went deeper than that before I could bring myself to ask you to marry me. You have to admit, it hardly seemed likely, considering that spot of retaliation you indulged in."

"I only did it because I thought you were going to do it to me again," Gina said softly. "I never got over the first time."

"Neither did I. I regretted it more than I've regretted anything in my life. I was telling the truth when I tricked you into coming to my hotel that first night. I had to see you again somehow and that was the only way without forcibly abducting you. I thought I'd left it too late when you told me you were getting married."

"Then you realised I wasn't as madly in love as I ought to be and started suspecting my motives." She gave a sigh. "I think you were probably more than half right. If I'd married Chris he'd have been getting by far the worst of the bargain." She turned her head a little to study the hard, lean profile, longing to have him reach out and take hold of her yet aware that things were still not clear between them. "Ryan, did you really intend us to live together out here?"

"Until I could be sure of your feelings for me, yes. Your coming at all went a long way considering what I'd said about the lack of security in the arrangement, but you seemed so cool about it all at the airport."

"I was only just beginning to fully appreciate what I'd done. I wasn't cool. I was all churned up inside and trying desperately not to let you see it." She put out an unsteady hand and touched his shoulder. "Ryan . . ." He looked at her for a long, soul-searching moment without moving, taking in the soft luminosity of her eyes, the tremulous curve of her lips, then his own face altered, the hardness dissolving as he drew her into his arms.

It was Ryan himself who finally and reluctantly called a temporary halt to abandonment, although he continued to hold her close, his lips against her hair. "I love you," he said, "and I want you, but not here like this. Not now." There was a smile in his voice. "Where would you like to go for your honeymoon? Just name it.

Gina said dreamily, "There's an island in the Bahamas that's just this side of Paradise."

He laughed softly. "Why this side?"

"Because there's nothing spiritual about the way you make me feel." She kissed the smooth tautness of his cheek, loving the male scent of his skin. "Anyway, that's where it all began, isn't it?"

"No," he said. "It all began days before then when a girl sat down at a table and looked at me with eyes like twin sapphires. I was planning on coming back to find her again the following week, but she forestalled me."

"And immediately put your back up."

"You could say that. I was punishing myself as well as you when I left you that night. I wanted you very badly."

"Such a strong will," she murmured, and felt him smile.

"That time for the wrong motives. You'd hit a couple of raw spots and it blinded me to everything else." He put her a little away from him to add on a note of quiet determination, "From now on I write the way I want to write without pandering to any public taste for extra titillation. I can afford to take the chance."

"I hope you're not thinking of cutting out sex altogether," she said in mock alarm, and received an equally mocking push of his fist against the side of her chin.

"Not where you're concerned for certain. I'm going to have a hard time writing this book when I do get round to it."

"No, you won't," she promised. "I'll be there when you want me, but I'll never interrupt at the wrong times. I'm going to be the perfect author's wife, darling, you just see."

"I can't wait." His expression changed a little. "It's going to take a couple of days or so to arrange a licence. I'll move my things across to one of the other rooms till then."

It was as much question as statement. Gina said softly, "Do we have to stay at the house after tonight? I want to go to the island with you, Ryan—*our* island. I want to swim with you in the lagoon, make love under the stars. We can come back to sign a few papers, can't we?"

"Wanton," he said. He was smiling. "Would you really trust me that far?"

"Why not? I'm going to be trusting you for a lifetime. You said it yourself once— there's no point in marriage unless you intend it to last. Ours is going to last, isn't it?"

He kissed her with passion and with love, hands tender. "You can count on it," he said.

*Other titles in the
Linford Series:*

## THE WAYWARD HEART
### by Eileen Barry

Disaster-prone Katherine's nickname was "Kate Calamity". She was a good natured girl, but her boss went too far with an outrageous proposal, because of her latest disaster, she could not refuse.

## FOUR WEEKS IN WINTER
### by Jane Donnelly

Tessa wasn't looking forward to going back to her old home town and meeting Paul Mellor again—she had made a fool of herself over him once before. But was Orme Jared's solution to her problem likely to be the right one?

## SURGERY BY THE SEA
### by Sheila Douglas

Medical student Meg hadn't really wanted to leave London and her boy-friend to go and work with a G.P. on the Welsh coast for the summer, although the job had its compensations. But Owen Roberts was certainly not one of them!

## HEAVEN IS HIGH
### by Anne Hampson

The new heir to the Manor of Marbeck had been found—an American from the Rocky Mountains! But it was rather unfortunate that when he arrived unexpectedly he found an uninvited guest, complete with Stetson and high boots, singing "I'm an old cowhand . . . Here I am, straight from those jolly ole Rockies . . ."

## LOVE WILL COME
### by Sarah Devon

June Baker's boss was not really her idea of her ideal man, but when she went from third typist to boss's secretary overnight she began to change her mind.

## ESCAPE TO ROMANCE
### by Kay Winchester

Oliver and Jean first met on Swale Island. They were both trying to begin their lives afresh, but neither had bargained for complications from the past.

## CASTLE IN THE SUN
### by Cora Mayne
Emma's invalid sister, Kym, needed a warm climate, and Emma jumped at the chance of a job on a Mediterranean island looking after another girl of Kym's age. But it wasn't that easy. Emma soon finds that intrigues and hazards lurk on the sunlit isle.

## BEWARE OF LOVE
### by Kay Winchester
Carol Brampton resumes her nursing career when her husband and daughter are killed in a car accident. With the help of Dr. Patrick Farrell she begins to pick up the pieces of her life, but is bitterly hurt when insinuations are made about her to Patrick.

## DESERT DOCTOR
### by Violet Winspear
Madeline felt that Morocco was a place made for love and romance, but unfortunately Doctor Victor Tourelle seemed to be unaffected by its romantic spell.